FAKIE

Fakie
Text © 2008 Tony Varrato

Published by Lobster Press™
1620 Sherbrooke Street West, Suites C & D
Montréal, Québec H3H 1C9
Tel. (514) 904-1100 • Fax (514) 904-1101 • www.lobsterpress.com

Publisher: Alison Fripp
Editors: Alison Fripp & Meghan Nolan
Editorial Assistants: Lindsay Cornish, Shiran Teitelbaum &
Lauren Clark
Graphic Design & Production: Tammy Desnoyers

Library and Archives Canada Cataloguing in Publication

Varrato, Tony, 1966-
    Fakie / Tony Varrato.

ISBN 978-1-897073-79-7

    I. Title.

PZ7.V378Fa 2008   j813'.6   C2007-905608-3

Printed and bound in Canada.

To Bonnie

– Tony Varrato

FAKIE

written by
Tony Varrato

Lobster Press ™

CHAPTER 1

IT WAS ALWAYS early morning when they left, and it was always in a different direction. As the car rolled quietly down the two-lane highway, he looked at his watch. 3:07 a.m. This time, they were headed south.

His mom broke the hour-long silence. "So, have you decided who you're going to be this time?"

He thought for a minute before answering. That's all he had been thinking about since they had left a half hour ago. But he had learned from everything that had happened so far that it was best to think before answering or acting. If he had done that in the first place, he and his mom wouldn't even be in this mess.

"I think I'd like to be a skateboarder."

"*Heh*, I guess you'll have to learn a new vocabulary. You'll be saying 'dude' and 'like' all the time."

"I don't think it'll be that bad. I'll need new clothes, though. I've been studying skateboarders on Ex-Tube. I need baggy pants, loose T-shirts, and Vans. And of course, a skateboard."

"How are you going to pull off the hair? You need it long and shaggy in front, don't you?"

He remembered that in his last life, he had been a jock and he buzzed off most of his hair with the rest of the team. Above all, he had to fit in.

"A lot of skateboarders and surfers shave their heads bald or close to it. I just might have to get a scalp tan so I don't look like a poser. What are you going to do?"

"I think I'll try being a redhead again. My hair's starting to get longer now. Maybe I'll get it straightened."

"You'd look good. Any idea of the job this time?"

"I want us to live within twenty minutes of the beach, so there should be lots of restaurants. Maybe a pizza joint this time."

His mom would only take jobs in restaurants. She needed as much on-hand cash as possible. They had to be ready to go at a moment's notice – just like tonight. There would be no time to hit the bank, and besides, the automatic bank machine left videos of each transaction. Pictures were a major mistake. That's why they were driving tonight.

He had shaved his head to fit in and had been cautious not to make any touchdowns. But he messed up and made a great tackle in last night's game. While his teammates and the crowd cheered, all he could think was: *What have I done?* The state newspaper ran his picture on the front page of the sports section that morning, so they had no choice but to leave as soon as it got dark.

Another life ended, a new one ready to begin. How many had this been? Seven? Eight? His real name didn't matter anymore. He could never be – and he didn't want to be – that person. That person was a jerk, a loser ... and worse; he hated that person. His mom was just *Mom*, he was her son, and Dad was gone. That's all there was to it.

"Do we have a last name yet?" he asked.

"How about Miller? It's common, but it's not too common."

"Great. I was afraid we were going to be in the Smith, Jones, and Johnson cycle again," he said.

"Hey, I'm getting better at this. I just hope we don't have to move too much more. I think I've only got ten social security numbers left."

"Well, if we get in a jam, we'll just have to call Mr. Lankford."

Mom was silent.

"As a last resort of course," he added.

"A very last resort," she said.

CHAPTER 2

THE STATE PRISON outside Chicago was a far cry from the gray, musty dungeons that Hollywood shows in all the multimillion-dollar movies. An ex-prisoner had made millions helping design this and other institutions with brighter colors and circular pods where the guards could watch all of the prisoners at one time if necessary. There were very few fights and no escape attempts. The prisoners were not happy to be there, but they knew they didn't run the place. The guards did.

Even so, Frank hated coming here. He could feel his heart speeding up at the possibility that he should be – and possibly could be – an inmate. It seemed as if he were a deer walking by the hunters. Worse yet, he was on his way to visit a lion.

Guards were stationed around the room, watching prisoners with their visitors at small tables. As he walked over to one of the tables, Frank shot a nervous glance at a guard not more than ten feet away. He realized that the guard didn't scare him as much as the man seated at the far table. The lion was out of his cage. As Frank sat down, a feeling of dread came over him. There were many ways Steve

Ballantine could reach Frank, even beyond the protective walls of the prison.

"Well?" Steve snarled. No *"Hello,"* *"Good to see you,"* or *"How's everybody?"* He was powerful, not friendly.

"Steve, we think we saw him in a paper in New York State three days ago. We've sent the girls there to check it out. He was playing football, and there was a big 5 X 7 of him on the front of the sports page."

Steve was patient until Frank finished. "You don't think they're stupid enough to stay there, do you?"

The words slashed like claws. Steve's tone, not his volume, clearly gave the message that Steve thought Frank was an idiot. Then again, according to Steve, everyone was an idiot.

"No, Steve, no. We figure they left already. But we'll do the usual search for clues with the other kids, the house, the job, and the bank. They have to slip up sometime."

"Let me know what you find." Steve took a long pause and lowered his voice. "I'm ready to try a new approach. Two years in this place is too much." He leaned forward in his chair, a new intensity blazing in his eyes. "I want them found."

Then, he leaned back in his chair and a smile spread across his face. "So, how's my business doing?"

CHAPTER 3

THREE DAYS WERE more than enough to set up a new life. Alex and Sonya Miller were now real people living nineteen minutes from the surf of Virginia Beach. They had a two-bedroom townhouse where Alex's mom had hooked up her computer, high-end printer, and scanner, which had all been provided by Mr. Lankford. Among other things, his mom had printed out a driver's license, social security cards, birth certificates, and – Alex's favorite – school records from any school in the country. He knew he could have a straight-A average if he wanted, but he had to blend in with the crowd. Bs were the perfect low-profile grades for a kid who needed to blend in to stay alive. Letters on a report card meant nothing to him. Alex knew he was smart enough to be at the top of any school he chose. His experiences in the past three-plus years had opened his eyes to a world very few other fifteen-year-olds had seen.

Even though he had gone through this procedure two previous times this school year, Alex was still nervous about his first day at a new school. He double-checked his new clothes to make sure that the dozen or so washings made them look as worn as possible. He felt like a poser, but then again, he always did. He tossed his backpack, with appropriate Alien Workshop and "Mean People Suck" patches, over one shoulder and headed out the door with Mom.

They opened the doors of their "new" 1988 white Toyota Tercel. They had sold their old car for scrap at a junkyard and bought the Tercel on their way through Delaware for eight hundred dollars cash. They liked buying old, boxy cars because no one ever bothered to steal anything from them. They weren't too exciting, but they ran forever. And besides – buying a rust bucket with cash doesn't leave a trail for anyone to follow.

When they pulled up to the school around 10:00 on that mid-November morning, the grounds were fairly deserted. The school day had begun, and most people were already in their classes. The Millers walked in and Alex quietly registered. Mrs. Wisniewski, the school secretary, was relieved that he had all of the paperwork with him so that she wouldn't have to play phone-tag with the other schools to get the information. Mrs. Wisniewski then entered his information into her database, printed out his schedule, and sent Alex off to his third period class.

Alex was always amazed that even before he had stepped into a classroom, everyone knew he was coming. The teachers sometimes knew, but the students had a communication network like no other. Just one student who saw something strange, like a new kid or a fight, could pass this information all over the school in less than sixty seconds. When word of mouth wasn't an option, text messaging sure got the job done. Alex had been in enough schools to know that cell phones were probably off-limits here, but that it didn't stop too many kids from sending messages under their desks.

When Alex opened the door and handed the history teacher his schedule, the rest of the class buzzed. The next two days would be difficult, but luckily, he saw a few others with the skater look. On his way to his seat, he gave his potential friends, who were seated in the back corner of the class, a head nod.

The teacher continued his lesson about the first winter in Jamestown. However, the class was really studying Alex that period. There were no eye rolls of disapproval, so he must have gotten his new look right. Also, some of the students checking him out were girls. He looked back at a few of them, but he didn't flirt or smile too much. It was too soon. He wished it were three days from now, when the newness was over.

He talked to a couple of boys casually between periods. He studied how they walked, the words they used, and their body language. Generally, these students didn't seem to be as hostile or defensive as the kids in some of his former schools. He was relieved.

The first jerk came along on the way back from lunch. Alex was lightly bumped, almost as if by accident. Then he heard, "Nice hair. You know they can fix baldness with hair plugs, right?" A large jock locked eyes with Alex as he slowly passed him in the crowded hall. A shark sizing up its prey.

"But he's got no hair to transplant. He's not man enough to have chest hair yet," added a skinnier jock with a high-pitched voice. Alex knew this type of idiot – he had been one of them just last week.

"Actually, I just shaved my chest this morning," replied Alex, puffing his chest and then running his fingers across his stubbly scalp. "I'm thinking of getting a hair weave."

The high-pitched boy cracked up, but the jerk refused to laugh. Alex could see that he wanted to though. "Oooh, New Kid thinks he's funny. Think again, chump."

In those few seconds, a small crowd had gathered to see if it was fight time. Alex knew better than to start anything; his first fake identity had been a tough guy. Too much publicity. Too many people wanted to test tough guys.

Alex swallowed the other wisecracks he had ready. He just smiled and turned toward class. As he walked into the room, he could feel the large jock's eyes burning a hole in his back.

This guy was going to be a problem, and Alex would have to deal with him soon. Above all, Alex had to blend in.

CHAPTER 4

IT WAS TIME for Alex to get serious. Since he had gotten out of the hospital, Alex had worked hard to get his body into some kind of shape. The doctor told him that there had been a lot of damage, but that exercise would help. Even after a year of weight lifting and jogging, he had had to put off a football identity because his body wasn't ready. He didn't want to be huge – he just wanted to be healthy, and because of his work, he was in fairly good shape. It was a good thing too; this was going to be a very physical identity. He had been looking at magazines, and the local video store had some helpful DVDs. So it was time to give skateboarding a try – privately.

Luckily, the townhouse his mom found had a garage. Because she tried to get the busy evening shifts as much as possible, he had the garage to himself until 10:00 p.m. or so. With the door closed, Alex put on pads and a helmet. He was pretty sure it was uncool to wear these things in public, but showing up at school with bandages was even more uncool. He picked up his new board. A guy in Ocean City had put it together for Alex so that he wouldn't look like a wannabe. The guy hooked him up with a

17

plain board with a slick bottom, and added trucks, bearings, and 60 mm starter wheels. Alex also bought some smaller wheels to use once he got the hang of it. The salesman said he could change the wheels himself when he was ready. That was fine with Alex – he liked fixing things with his hands.

Alex put his right foot behind the front hardware and pushed off with his left. There wasn't much room in the single-car garage, so he had to practice carving. He leaned left and right. That seemed easy enough, but he had to keep doing it until he felt comfortable.

Once he had that down, it was time to practice his ollie. He slammed his back foot on the tail of the deck and jumped. Nothing. This would obviously take a lot more work.

His mother came home at about 11:00 p.m. By that time, Alex was doing homework and listening to Rage Against the Machine on his MP3 player.

She fluffed her newly dyed red hair, laughed, and dropped her apron on the chair. "Well, how did it go?"

"It was a typical first day. I dressed right, the teachers seem okay, and I met the first bully, I think."

"What are you going to do about him?" she asked.

"The usual."

CHAPTER 5

FRANK SAT DOWN at the prison visiting table and spoke to Steve quietly. "You were right." He figured Steve wasn't going to say hello anyway, so he might as well get down to business. "Nothing. We found out the type of car and the license plate number, but she's ditched that car already." He leaned in, just a little closer. "So, what's your new idea?"

"I need a map," Steve said. "Mark every place we know they've stayed and make sure we have every move accounted for. Disguise it as papers from my lawyer or something – do whatever you've gotta do to get that map in here. I want to know everywhere they've been." He locked his predatory eyes on Frank and spoke slowly, clearly. "No gaps."

"I don't think there are any gaps, but I'll double-check."

"Do that. There has to be an underlying pattern to their movements." Steve gritted his teeth. "It would be nice for you guys to figure out where they are now, instead of always being one step behind."

* * *

Day two is always the worst, Alex thought. You're still the new kid, but now everyone wants to get all of the information they can about you. Of course, Alex could not tell anyone anything about himself or about his past lives. There could be no connecting him with who he really was. Alex remembered an old song his dad used to play, where the singer cried, "You can't hide from yourself!" Alex, who was not really Alex, was determined to prove that singer wrong.

Thinking about the song brought up memories he didn't want to deal with. A brief image of his dad singing terribly as usual. Mom telling him he sounded like someone stepped on a cat. Happy memories. Then other memories flashed at him: the explosion of the gun and the silent scream.

I'm sorry, Dad.

He shook away his tears. Alex had to get into character and pretend to be normal. He had to bluff his way through this identity, like he did with all the others.

He had invented a stock lie that only had to be modified slightly with each move. He realized that by using this lie, he was assuming he wasn't staying in one place for long. It was realistic, but depressing as hell. It would be so nice to finally stay somewhere, to be himself. Unfortunately, he did not know exactly who that was anymore.

A boy with hair past his shoulders stopped in front of Alex in the hallway. "If you read that in class, the teachers'll take it from you," he said.

The wrinkled skate magazine in Alex's hand worked like a charm. "Yeah, that's because secretly, they're all skate punks," Alex replied.

"Yeah, especially Mr. Jackson. I bet at night, when no one's around, that old guy's shredding on the handrails and the front stairs!"

They both laughed, and with that, Alex made his first friend in this life.

"My name's Tim."

"I'm Alex."

"Yeah, I know. You're in three of my classes."

"Cool."

"Well, I've gotta get – "

"Hey!" a loud voice boomed from behind them. The jock from the day before shoved his way between Tim and Alex. "Skate wuss and turtle head. You two look cute together." The jock puffed up his shoulders and walked confidently into Tim's class.

"Give us a kiss," squeaked the high-pitched sidekick, as he squeezed past them.

Alex and Tim watched and fumed for a moment.

They both just shook their heads. Alex turned to Tim and asked, "Who's the caveman, and what's with his little sidekick?"

"The loud one's Brian, and his buddy's Carl. They give everybody crap. You just get an extra dose because you're new."

Alex nodded.

"I'd like to whack him in the back of the head and stick him in a locker, but he probably wouldn't fit. What a freakin' buffalo." Tim shook his head and gathered his books.

As the bell rang, Alex realized he liked Tim already. Most of the kids he had met would have been ticked off for the rest of the day after an exchange like that. Tim was smart enough to brush off stupid comments and get on with his life.

"So, where does ol' Brian live?" Alex asked his new friend.

"He lives only about a mile from here. He likes to hang around after basketball and torment the little kids at the middle school next door," Tim replied rolling his eyes.

"That figures."

"Why do you care?"

"Just curious. That's all."

CHAPTER 6

IMAGES FLICKER IN *the boy's mind like a silent movie. Two men yell. The gun flashes. No one hears the scream.*

"Alex."

Alex leapt up from the sofa. "I must've dozed off." He rubbed his foggy eyes.

"You don't have to wait up for me every night, you know," his mother said.

"Yeah, I know," he answered, now fully awake. "I just feel better knowing you're home."

"I know what you mean," she replied. "I feel the same way while you're at school. I'm always afraid this'll be the day someone finds out." She flopped down onto the sofa next to him. "So, how was school? How is practice going?"

"Practice is going well. I finally have the ollie down, which is awesome, but I need some more work on my kickflip. School's okay. The classes are pretty much the same as at the other schools, but the bully is still giving me grief. I get the feeling he's going to take a swing at me soon, which will lead to a fight, which I really don't want or need right now." Alex sighed.

"You know that you need to be careful," she said sternly. "Remember, we had to leave our second identity because you hung around with bullies. That got very messy, very quickly."

"Yeah," Alex confessed. "I thought about that." His eyes glazed over as he remembered another life full of fights, insults, and anger. He blinked and he was back in Virginia Beach. "I didn't like who I turned into there for a while either. I want to handle this quickly and quietly."

His mother shot him that warning glare that all mothers seem to know.

"I'm only going to talk to him." He raised his hands in defense.

Sonya sighed. "Just be careful." She put her hand on his shoulder. "Now, it's time for bed."

* * *

"Hey, Alex, what are you doing after school?" Tim asked on the way to homeroom the next morning.

"Not much. Why?"

"Me, Nate, and Tyler are going to build a skate ramp in my backyard."

"Cool! You mean a big one?"

"Yeah, pretty big. We're using some old wood and stuff. My dad's got tons of tools. We just need to figure out how to build the thing."

The word "dad" still hit Alex like a punch, even after all this time. He shook it off and hoped his face didn't show any emotion.

"Sounds good. What time?"

"We're going right after school. Do you need to ask your parents?"

"Yeah," Alex said. "I'll ask, but it'll be all right."

"You bike to school, so you can just follow us over."

"Maybe just give me the directions. I have to help my mom first since we're still moving in and all. But I'll be right over afterwards. Will you guys still be going around 5:30?"

"Yeah, my mom's getting pizza, so we can work through dinner."

As they walked through the classroom door, Alex said, "I'll be there." He couldn't stop smiling.

* * *

Basketball ended that day at 5:00. By 5:07, Brian and his crew were harassing the sixth graders at the middle school. The usual stuff: pushing them, throwing their shoes on top of the overhang in front of the gym entrance – "accidentally," of course – and daring the sixth graders to do something about it.

Finally, when the last friend left, and the last fuming sixth grader had gone home to sulk, Brian started his walk home. He cut across the parking lot and stomped through the flower bed, ignoring the sidewalk. This would lead him to the other side of the school and then to the woods.

Something moved in the corner of Brian's eye, but he didn't have a chance to recognize it. He was already on the ground holding his stomach, gasping for breath.

"That's your solar plexus, Brian."

"Auhh," Brian groaned.

"Don't try to talk or get up." Alex spoke quietly, but pointedly, as if he had done this before. "There are five other pressure points I can hit without leaving a mark. Wanna see?"

"Nauhh!"

"Good. Now, I don't want to have any more trouble with you. If I do, I'll have to show you one of the other five points. And I'll do this someplace public, like in the hallway." He paused and took a deep breath. "I don't plan on mentioning this to anyone if you don't. Got me?"

"Auhh."

"Good. I'll see ya around."

Alex breathed a sign of relief as he slipped onto his bike. *That was almost too easy*, he thought. He believed that he had convinced Brian not to bother him anymore. If he could convince his new friends that he was a skater, then he could relax a little.

He left Brian, who was finally starting to breathe normally, cowering under a shrub.

* * *

"Denver, Colorado; Macon, Tennessee; Minneapolis, Minnesota; Fort Worth, Texas; Rosette, Utah; Phoenix, Arizona; Caneadea, New York," recited Frank, pointing at a map in a copy of *National Geographic*. The locations were only faintly dotted, invisible to the guards, who had to inspect all materials going into and coming out of the prison. Frank double-checked the chronological list he hid in the text of the phony lawyer documents. "There's no real pattern," he said to Steve.

Steve studied the magazine map with the faint dots marking the towns. "Use Google Earth to zoom down and look for their car! Access their satellites and follow them from New York!" he demanded.

Frank took a deep breath to hide his frustration. "It doesn't work like that," he explained. "Google Earth's satellite pictures are months, sometimes years old. They don't show live action."

"Don't we have someone who can get us live

pictures?" Steve barked.

Frank sighed. "We're working on it. We're negotiating with someone now. But even when we have this guy's help, we're still looking at months needed to access old footage from many different satellites." He shook his head. "It could take longer than we have."

"Then you'd better find a pattern before my appeal date."

"I told you," Frank blurted. "City, small town, city, city ... There *is* no pattern."

"But," Steve interjected with his usual condescending tone, "that's the pattern. It's too random. There has to be some plan behind each move." He sharpened his next words with sarcasm and threw them like daggers. "If there were no plan, I'd like to think that you would be able to catch them."

"So, what do we do? Just guess their next stop?" Frank was getting desperate.

"No," Steve glared. "We look at the areas they haven't been yet. That would be this area here."

"The East Coast? That doesn't narrow it down much," Frank protested.

"It does, since they have already been up north. They will go someplace in the middle here, like Maryland, Virginia, or the Carolinas."

"Four states is a lot to cover," argued Frank.

"That's why you're going to need some help from the girls, and maybe even some help from the FBI." Steve's voice was low with contempt. "Here's what you're going to do. Write this down, so you don't forget."

CHAPTER 7

TOM LANKFORD HAD been with the Federal Bureau of Investigation for twenty-seven years. His first eleven were spent in the Drug Enforcement Agency. He really liked the job, especially the adrenaline rush he got when bullets went whizzing past his head during a raid. Eventually, though, he realized that he couldn't bear the thought of widowing his wife and leaving his kids without a father.

Since then, Lankford, known only by his last name, worked in conjunction with the U.S. Marshals Service in the Witness Protection Program. It wasn't as dangerous as it had been in the field, but the covert nature of his work excited him. He loved making up names and histories; with his computer, he could easily create legitimate birth certificates, death certificates, marriage certificates, college transcripts, and social security numbers. He felt like a magician, making people appear and disappear.

He told no one about his clients and kept whatever information he shared with his superiors to a bare minimum. It was the surest way to keep them alive; after all, there had been leaks in the department before. But for the last sixteen years, he had never lost a client. He was their protector, their lifeline.

Often, he arranged e-mail contact with his clients to protect them from phone traces, but recently, ISP identification had become more sophisticated. Even with potentially anonymous web e-mail systems, like Yahoo and Hotmail, it was possible to track the user to a specific computer. For these reasons, Lankford advised his clients to only contact him in case of emergency.

"Okay then," Lankford whispered to himself in his isolated office as he shut down his computer for the day. No one needed his lifeline today.

He stood, stretching his body, which was slightly overweight from too much chair time. Lankford packed his junk mail into his briefcase and walked to the front door of the building.

"Goodnight," he said to the security guard in the hall.

"Goodnight, Lankford."

He fumbled for his keys on the walk to his car. The former field agent stopped and scanned the area for any sign of danger, and with a little sadness, saw none.

He let out a sigh; he missed the drug raids.

Many cars away, Lankford's killer watched him through binoculars as he got into his car and headed home to his wife and kids.

CHAPTER 8

"DUDE, WE SHOULD add some rails so we can grind!" declared Nate. His hair, which was only long in the front, usually hit the tip of his nose, so he spent the majority of his time flicking it back.

"Are you slackers done yet, or what?" Alex needled. He dropped his bike and walked toward his friends.

"Hardly," Tim said, looking at Alex, then at his watch, then back at Alex. He looked as if he was going to ask Alex a question, but decided not to. "This ramp is turning into an amusement park."

"Well, if we're going to do this," added Tyler, "I say we build a killer half-pipe and a couple of rails, or we just go back to jumping soda cans in the driveway."

"I've got a question," Alex said. "Isn't there a skate park, like, ten miles down the road?"

"Yeah," Nate admitted, "and it's pretty cool. But roller bladers and BMXers use it too, so it gets totally crowded. And it takes half an hour to get there."

"And," Tyler butted in, "we want to shred everyday. So that bike ride each day after school cuts into our time. Plus, there's changing, packing stuff ..."

"Listen to you talk about shredding," joked Nate.

"You couldn't even pull off an ollie a minute ago! You looked like a jumping bean, but the board never left the ground! Boing. Boing. Boing."

"Dude, I make one mistake and you – "

"Anyway," Tim interrupted loudly, "this is turning into a huge project. The half-pipe alone will be thirty-six feet long. I'm gonna have to ask my mom if we can add all this other stuff. Plus, we're going to have to get more wood and some really heavy poles."

"Well, if it's cool with your mom, we could all chip in to buy the stuff," Alex suggested.

Tim pushed his hair out of his eyes and stared at the space where the skate ramp would be. Alex noticed that Nate and Tyler waited for an answer, as if he were a judge. "That could work," he mused, still staring at the space. "I figure we'll need one low, level rail and another one on an incline. They'll have to be sturdy, maybe galvanized." He turned to face his friends. "They won't be cheap."

"Maybe we can check out a junkyard, if you have one around here," Alex suggested. "Or maybe some yard sales? People always sell the strangest stuff, like broken axles from their trucks. They're like, 'Hey, wanna buy my old toilet? It doesn't work, but you can plant some nice flowers in it.'"

The boys laughed. "You're messed up, dude!" crowed Nate.

Alex tried to hide his pride. He was in.

"You know what we should do?" offered Nate. "We should take Alex to Mount Trashmore on Saturday, so he can see what we're going for."

"Excellent idea! Alex, are you up for it?" asked Tim.

Alex smiled. He really wanted to be one of them. But he knew it couldn't last. It never did. "Saturday's great."

* * *

The secretary at Anne Arundel High School in Maryland looked up as she put down the handset of her steadily ringing phone. "Hello. Can I help you?" she offered in a friendly voice, which didn't reveal how her nerves had thinned with each ring of her phone.

"Yes, my name is Rachel Phillips and I'm from the Department of Education," lied Gina, dressed in a nice, but easily forgettable, blue suit. "I need some information about any new students who have enrolled within the last month."

"Why? Is there a problem?"

"No," continued Gina. "DOE is testing a new student record system, and I'm spot-checking schools and student transfers under the current record systems. I'm really just surveying."

"Well, our guidance counseling office is the second door on the right. Good luck with your work."

"Thanks." Gina smiled and gave a slight tilt of her head. *Good luck is right*, she said to herself. This was the first of five schools that she had to visit today alone. It could take months to find that little punk!

CHAPTER 9

ALEX KNEW HE was out of his league. He had been practicing like crazy in the garage over the last three nights with makeshift ramps – ollieing over cans, just as Nate had joked. "Every joke contains some truth," one of his counselors used to say. So he figured it wasn't a bad idea to learn how to jump things. He had searched the Internet at the library for skateboarding tricks and he found a site called "Basic Tricks Every Beginner Should Know." He hadn't perfected them, but at least he had tried a few. Saturday's trip could expose him for the fake he was. He was going to have to confess to his friends that he wasn't very good. After all, he *had* only been a skateboarder for a week.

It was a good thing the counselors forced him to get into shape by training on a stationary bike while he was in the hospital. He was a strong rider, so Mom was happy to let him bike to Virginia Beach on Saturday morning, even though they had planned a lot of biking. They would pedal to the beach, hang out there for a while, and then go to the skate park for the rest of the day. Mom told him to be careful and gave him a kiss – in front of his friends. But then she slid him forty bucks, which almost made the kiss okay.

When they approached Atlantic Avenue, Alex was in the lead. He could see the ocean and he was excited. They chained their bikes near a pizza shop, which was closed for a couple more hours, and grabbed their skateboards. Surprisingly, the streets were fairly deserted, even on this warm November day.

Today, the sidewalks were reserved for skateboarders and roller bladers. Guys with body piercings and huge tattoos of crosses on their backs were ollieing off the curbs and landing smoothly in the empty side streets.

"Come on," said Nate. "Let's go to the boardwalk."

First of all, the boardwalk was cement. Second of all, it took Alex several minutes to realize that. Instead, he noticed girls walking around in less clothing than they wore in the other towns he had lived in.

"Dude," interjected Tyler. "Haven't you been to the beach before?"

"Uh, no," replied Alex, turning red for the second time this morning. "I haven't."

"Okay, but try not to stare. You're a local now."

Alex nodded. "Let's skate."

They began skating down the bike path, which was paved and flat. They jumped some curbs and ollied over a few cement parking blocks. Nate showed Alex how to stall on the blocks. "Ya gotta learn to get your balance before you can grind," he explained.

Alex practiced it a few times while the others tried some hardflips. *That looks painful*, he thought. *I'm definitely not there yet.*

At 10:30, they grabbed some burgers and then went into a skate shop.

"I like these long decks," Alex stated.

"They're like surfboards, though," Tim told him. "You've gotta work up to the longer ones."

"Do you guys surf too?" Alex asked, feeling like a huge tourist.

"No," replied Tim. "But there's an awesome surf camp up in Delaware. You stay all week and have campfires and stuff. My mom said I can go this summer if I get a job to pay for it."

"That sounds cool."

"If you guys are up for it, maybe we can all go," Tim suggested.

Alex nodded. A second later, he realized he had made his first long-term promise in three years. He hoped he could keep it.

At about 11:00, they biked out to the skate park. Alex was expecting a couple of ramps and maybe a half-pipe. He was shocked and a little intimidated by what he saw.

Alex looked around at the huge bowl and the massive street course. "We don't have to pay to get in?"

"Right. It's huge, isn't it? And it's a landfill. That's why it's named Mount Trashmore. They dumped a ton of garbage, covered it up, and made it a park." Tyler said grinning. "We're gonna thrash on the trash!"

"Cool," agreed Alex.

"Let's hit the bowl first," yelled Nate, as soon as they locked up their bikes.

"Dude!" Tyler whipped out his cell phone and yelled to Nate. "Let's video each other for YouTube."

"Cool!"

The thought of dropping into the seven-foot-deep bowl freaked Alex out, so he decided to spend time on the street course. Watching other skaters, he tried some grabs and ollies over ramp spines. When he landed his first frontside 180, he let out a "Yes!"

He looked around, but no one else was paying attention. No big deal – Alex knew it wasn't a historical milestone like Tony Hawk's 900, but it felt as if he had just conquered the world. Today, he was a little less of a fake. The world was a little less scary.

He looked up at the bowl defiantly. *Soon*, he promised himself, *I'll drop in*.

CHAPTER 10

"HEY, WHAT'S UP?" Tim asked, as he pulled his bike into the school bike rack.

Alex clicked his lock closed and looked up. "It's Monday morning," he announced in mock enthusiasm. "Just getting ready for another exciting day of learning."

"Uh, okay then," Tim answered with a laugh. "Are you sore from Saturday?" He locked his bike and they walked toward the school.

"Yeah, a little," Alex confessed. "Mostly my legs and my butt."

Tim nodded. "Totally. And my sides are wrecked too. I think I might have overdone the bowl."

As they relived the high points of Saturday, Alex realized how much better this identity felt than the others. No one harassed him about not going into the bowl. His new friends felt like *real* friends. It even felt, Alex thought, as if he could finally open up and be himself. Well, as open and himself as a person could be when he was forced to lie about nearly every detail of his life.

However, Alex was bothered by a suspicion that he had – that Tim knew he had been lying all along. Tim didn't talk endlessly, like Nate and Tyler; he only spoke when he had something to say. He was the kind of guy whose wheels were always turning. It had been obvious all week that Tim had something to say to Alex, but that he kept stopping short of saying it. Alex was afraid that it was just a matter of time before Tim called him a poser.

"Ooof!" grunted some poor daydreaming kid on his way to science. Alex thought his name was John.

"Pay attention, dork," growled Brian as he bumped John into an open locker. Brian's dopey grin faded for a second as his eyes locked with Alex's. Then his usual cocky face returned and he strutted into class.

"What was that?" asked Tim catching the stare-down contest.

"I guess Brian just chose John for his victim of the day."

"That's not what I meant."

"What?"

"The staring thing?" prompted Tim. "Come to think of it, Brian stopped picking on you pretty quick after you first got here. What's up?"

Alex puffed up his chest and lowering his voice said, "I guess he just knows I'd kick his butt!"

"Yeah," Tim added sarcastically. "I'm sure

that's it." Tim stared at Alex for another second or two. He obviously had something else to say, but he held back.

"All right, everyone. Let's take our seats," Mr. Henry announced.

Alex briefly saw a kid named Mike take something from behind his back and place it in the trash can – gently, but quickly. *Strange*, thought Alex as he got out his science book.

It took three full minutes before the firecrackers went off, blowing trash in the air and sending most of the students under their desks – at least the ones who had common sense. Mike had common sense. Brian did not.

Mr. Henry took cover behind his desk. Then he looked up and saw the only student who barely moved – obviously, the guilty one. "Brian Joseph! Go down to the office right now! I'll send the referral down after you!"

"Me? What did I do?"

"Oh, come now, Mr. Joseph! You're the only one who didn't duck! You knew it was coming, and if you didn't set off the firecracker, you know who did! Now either tell me who it was, or leave immediately!"

"This is crap!" protested Brian.

"No," answered his teacher. "Arson is crap.

And arson is the charge you'll get for setting off firecrackers on school property. The school may bring charges against you, and you might be arrested. At bare minimum, you'll probably be suspended or expelled. That was not a wise thing to do, Brian!"

"I didn't do it!"

The class was silent. Brian stood alone, waiting for someone to help him. The rest of the students had come out from under their desks and were back in their seats. They didn't laugh, as they normally would have after a prank. Instead, they stared accusingly at Brian. *They all think he's guilty! No, not all*, Alex realized. Mike had a faint smile on his face.

The whispering started when Brian left. While Mr. Henry wrote up the office referral, the students held court. "Good! I'm glad he's finally gone." "It's about time!" "Jerk!"

"That was nuts! D'ya think he's gonna be back?" Tim whispered.

"Yeah," Alex whispered back. "Because he didn't do it. And, lucky me, I get to sneak down to the office and save his butt."

"You've gotta be kidding me! What are you talking about?" Tim's whisper was now a hoarse, muffled yell.

"*Shhhh!* I watched Mike put it in the trash can."

"Why didn't you say something sooner?"

"I ... uh ... I'm the new kid, and I don't need anybody thinking I'm a narc."

"I didn't think you cared that much about what other people thought."

"Would you believe that I don't want people to think I'm friends with that idiot?"

"Yeah, that I'll buy," smiled Tim. "Don't you want to wait and let Brian squirm a little?"

"Oh, definitely," agreed Alex. "I didn't say I was in any big rush."

* * *

The killer peered through his binoculars as Lankford kissed his wife and got into his car. Aaron marked down: "Tuesday, November 23, 7:38 a.m.: Leaves for work."

He let Lankford drive off for a full minute before following. He knew where his target was going, so there was no need to risk being seen. Lankford would stop at WaWa, a local convenience store, to grab a cappuccino, a coffee cake, and a paper. Aaron knew Lankford would drive cautiously to work. "Cautiously" was the key word: every few seconds, this paranoid cop would glance around, looking for guys who were waiting to jump him. Spending your time trying to avoid an attack was a pretty pathetic way to make yourself feel important. Unfortunately for Lankford, those fears were going to become a reality.

CHAPTER 11

WHEN GYM STARTED at the beginning of the second semester in late January, it felt like spring with its sunny, slightly breezy 72°F. In the two months he had been here, Alex still hadn't completely adjusted to the warm winter – his brain kept insisting that it was cold outside. When the holidays ended, Alex had expected a brutally cold winter waiting for him, forcing him to stay inside. But that just wasn't the case. He quickly learned to appreciate the warmth, especially when he had time to work on the skate ramp with his friends.

Having gym outside in January was always pretty cool, though "required showering" never was – especially for Alex. In the shower, others could see his scars, and that would lead to rumors and questions.

The locker room echoed with loud voices. A couple of boys rolled their towels and rat-tailed other kids as they came out of the showers. When the gym teacher finally arrived, his only comment was, "Everybody gets a shower, or points will be taken off your grade."

As always, Alex stalled until most of the others

were hurrying to get out of the locker room. Then he kept his back to the shower wall and covered his chest scars with soap lather as quickly as possible. He was showered and dressed within minutes.

He ran his fingers through his hair in the mirror. He was letting it grow a little longer now, mostly in the front, like Tyler's. Above all, he had to fit in. And if winter ever did come this year, a shaved head would be very cold. The locker room got suddenly quiet as the gym door closed and cut off the hall noise. Alex had to hurry.

"Miller!"

On the outside, Alex didn't flinch, but on the inside, his stomach was doing somersaults.

It was Brian, and they were the only two people in the locker room.

"Just so you know, I know you were the one who helped me out of the firecracker crap a couple months ago. I've been thinking a lot about it, and it had to be you. I could tell by the look on your face before I left Henry's room. I just wanted to finally say thanks."

"Don't worry about it," Alex answered without a smile. He couldn't have Brian thinking he was soft. "You didn't do it, so there was no reason for you to get nailed. But don't go thinking this makes us friends or anything."

"Of course not," Brian said, as both boys turned toward the door. The next class would be starting soon. "I don't want any skate punk friends."

"Fine by me. So hey, when you're not beating people up, what do you do for fun?"

"I ride my four-wheeler through the woods."

"Oh yeah? I used to do that," Alex admitted. "A friend of mine had one that could race at eighty miles an hour, and he tried to use it to jump ditches. He broke both of his arms – looked like a cactus with his casts on."

Brian laughed. "I've got one that races too. I've never broken my arms, but I've come pretty close – I've flipped it a couple of times." He paused a moment before they opened the hallway door. "You can come over and try to break your arms sometime if you want."

Alex smiled. "Yeah, that'd be cool."

As they entered the hallway with the rest of the students, Brian's expression and tone returned to normal. "Of course we're still not friends."

"Of course not!"

* * *

The best time to go to a pizza restaurant is Monday at 3:30. The weekend is gone, lunch has been over for a while, and even early dinner customers won't show up for at least an hour. It was the perfect time for Alex, Tim, Nate, and Tyler to talk to Alex's mom without making her manager mad. The hostess sat them immediately in Alex's mom's section. His mother was just finishing up another table's order.

"And I'd like the cheeseburger platter," said the customer.

"How would you like that cooked, sir?"

"Medium-well. And it's important that I don't get a pickle. If you even put the pickle on my plate and then take it off, the juice could get on my fries and I could eat it. Then my tongue would swell up, and you'd have to take me to the hospital."

"I gotcha," his mother replied sweetly. "I'll personally make sure no pickle even touches your plate. Will there be anything else?"

Everyone at the table shook their heads, and she went to get their drinks.

Two minutes later, Alex's mom came to their table. "Hey, boys. What are you up to this afternoon?"

"We're on our way to Tim's house, and we thought we'd stop by to get some pickles," Alex joked.

"I'd like to gargle with a pickle-juice cocktail, please," added Tyler.

"You are a strange young man, Tyler," his

mother laughed.

"Thanks, Mrs. Miller," said Tyler with a big grin.

"Mom, can you take us to the junkyard sometime? We've finished everything, but we still need to get the rails."

"I'll double-check my schedule, but I think I could do it on a Saturday morning."

"Thank you, Mrs. Mil-ler," sang Tyler in his best second-grade voice.

* * *

Wa Wa, 7:48, Tuesday morning. Lankford slid his three bucks across the counter and pocketed his change. He sipped the hot French vanilla cappuccino and singed his tongue as he did every morning. Before shouldering the door open, he glanced around the store, just as he did every day. With his coffee and cake in his left hand and his newspaper tucked under his left arm, his right hand was always free to reach for his gun if he had to. He walked to his car, scanning the parking lot. He unlocked his door as a light blue Honda pulled into the spot next to him. The driver got out and trudged into the store to get his own caffeine fix.

Lankford had already slid into his seat and closed his door when he noticed his rear-view mirror was pointing all the way up so that he could not see the back seat. Almost immediately, he felt the gun barrel in the back of his neck.

"Start the car and drive your normal route. I need to talk to you," Aaron directed in a low, calm voice. "Keep both hands on the steering wheel. You're not fast enough to get that nine-millimeter out of its holster before I mess up your windshield, so don't bother trying."

Lankford knew better than to say anything. Scan. Look for a way out. Another policeman? A place to jump out? Slam on the brakes?

"Now," Aaron said, his voice still low and almost soothing, "since I've been watching you for a couple months, I feel like I know you. You're thinking of trying to jump out, to signal someone for help, or something like that. Bad idea. If you do, I'll have to visit your lovely wife and two children." He paused for effect. "By the way, I think it's really sweet the way she hands you a packed lunch every day."

Lankford's breath caught in his throat. The car pulled onto the 25 mph residential road leading to the FBI office.

"So let's talk," responded Lankford, less calmly than he wanted to.

"I need Danny Torbert's address. See? Nothing too tricky."

"I haven't had contact with them in over a year!"

"Okay, watch that speed. We're in a 25 zone here," Aaron cautioned. "Tell me where they are and how you contact them."

Lankford paused. "They contact me only if they need me. I have no idea where they are."

"Tell me how to contact them." Aaron's voice was still quiet but sounded impatient. "Give me phone numbers, e-mails, passwords, or anything you've set up to communicate with them."

Silence.

"Oh, come on," Aaron scoffed. "I've had hackers working on this since we found you. They'll probably get the information anyway in a couple more weeks, but I'm in a hurry." His voice lowered to a whisper. "Help me out and you'll live. If not, the hackers'll find it anyway, and then you'll have died for nothing. Save us all some trouble. Save yourself."

"No." Dozens of lives were at stake here – not just Danny's and Eileen's, but all of the lives that had been entrusted to him. Lankford no longer missed the drug raids; he missed his family.

"Are you sure? Your wife and kids?"

Lankford shook his head.

Aaron pulled the trigger, which did, in fact, mess up the windshield. Aaron then opened the door and rolled onto the sidewalk as Lankford's car cruised into oncoming traffic.

Aaron brushed himself off as the light blue Honda stopped to pick him up. Lankford's car smashed into an oncoming pickup truck. He ignored the series of tire squeals and crashes that followed as he slid into the passenger seat.

"Anything?" Frank asked.

"No. Guess we call Echelon."

"It figures. Want your coffee?"

CHAPTER 12

THE NEXT MORNING in history class, everything changed.

"Current events. Your life is affected by things happening around you every day, whether you're paying attention or not," Mr. O'Neil recited for the nineteenth time that year. "You'd better start paying attention." Two students mouthed the words as they slapped a copy of *USA Today* on each desk.

Centered and in full color, the photo of the smashed cars caught Alex's eyes first. As the words in the headline came into focus, his breath was wrung from his body: "FBI Officer Shot, Others Dead in Car Wreck."

Like a gas explosion, the memories flashed in his brain. *The gunshots. The falling body. The silent scream.*

* * *

Alex didn't exist. However, an eleven-year-old named Danny Torbert lived in the suburbs of Chicago. On weekends, he and his family would go to parks, ride bikes, and play board games in Dad's office. During the week, everyone was busy. Danny rode his bike to school. Eileen, his mom, worked at the bank. Rick, his dad, worked, but Danny had never been exactly sure what that work was. Danny asked once, and his dad told him he repaired computers.

However, when Dad's work friends came over occasionally, and Danny was shooed upstairs to his room so that they could have "adult time," Danny heard differently. He picked up quietly spoken phrases like "call detail records" and "vibration sensor." Danny had used computers enough to know that those words didn't seem as if they had much to do with computer repair. It seemed to Danny that his dad's business was more about surveillance. Who was he watching? And why was the business kept so secret that Danny had to go upstairs?

Rick would always apologize to Danny after his co-workers left. He didn't like to bring work home, but sometimes it was important. Rick's business partner, Steve, was the one who came over the most. He was always friendly with Danny, with his booming, "Hey, Buddy! How's it goin'?" The loud behavior, which had scared Danny when he was younger, became more comfortable as he got used to the man. Danny and Steve would even give each other high fives before Danny was politely dismissed.

Rarely, maybe once every few months, other men would come over too. Danny didn't remember them very well. Once, just once, a tall, thin man came with Steve. That day, Rick rushed to the door.

"I told you I don't want him in my house!" Rick yelled at Steve. In the brief argument that followed, Danny found out that the other man's name was Aaron. Danny had never seen his dad angry like that before. Maybe it was his dad's reaction. Maybe it was the look in Aaron's eyes. Whatever the reason, Danny had nightmares about the tall, thin man for weeks.

Looking back, Danny realized that while Aaron would later be part of his real-life nightmare, he wasn't the architect of the nightmare. That was someone else.

The day it happened started out perfectly. It was sunny, warm for Illinois in the fall. There was a half day at school. To top it off, Dad was going to take him to a park that had just installed a new rock wall and bungee swing. Danny wasted no time riding his bike past the crossing guards and down the few short blocks to his home.

When he saw Steve's car in the driveway, the

air seemed to go out of Danny's tires, along with his hopes for the day.

Adult time.

Disappointed, Danny went around the back of the house to use the sliding door so that he wouldn't make noise and interrupt their meeting.

As he opened the door, he realized there was no reason to be quiet. He could hear them yelling at one another.

"I don't see why you're being such a jerk about this!" Steve yelled.

"Because the guy is guilty!" Dad shouted. "We've been watching him for months. I heard some of the phone recordings from less than an hour ago!"

"So did I ... and so did the rest of the team!" Steve defended. "And we certainly haven't heard any proof that he has any connection to terrorists!"

Dad raged. "What are you talking about? The conversations are perfectly clear. He talks about guns, money, dates, and times. This guy is working with terrorists! There is no question whatsoever!" Suddenly, Dad got quiet. "Unless someone altered the tape ..." Dad's voice got a little louder. "Wait, I've got a duplicate of the audio right here."

Danny tried to understand the conversation about phone taps, photographic evidence, and weapon sales that followed, but it flew past him. He had never heard yelling and cursing like this in his life and he was scared.

Danny picked up the phone to call Mom – she'd know what to do. But he hesitated because he remembered the rule: when Steve was here, Danny was supposed to go to his room. He should be upstairs with his door shut – he shouldn't even be down here. Danny decided that he was just overreacting, and that Dad was just having an argument with Steve. Adults argued sometimes. That's all there was to it.

Danny put down the phone.

His dad yelled, "Then let's just listen to the rest of it! It's right there in the audio!"

Danny could hear a recorded voice, but he couldn't hear the words.

"Right there!" his dad roared. "Did you hear that? He's buying weapons."

Steve said something Danny couldn't hear over the audio.

There was a pause, and then his dad yelled, "Did he just say your name?"

Danny turned the phone on again and punched the first few numbers of the bank, since Mom usually turned off her cell at work. But then the voices in the office grew quiet.

It's okay now, he told himself. *Everything is fine*. He hung up the phone.

He hovered at the office door, trying to hear inside.

"How could you do it, Steve? How could you betray your own country?" Rick yelled.

Steve's voice remained quiet. Danny could only hear him murmur.

His dad's voice was still loud and clear. "You're working for him, aren't you? You're selling him weapons and covering it up, aren't you?"

Steve murmured.

"You and who else? Frank? Aaron?" Rick accused.

Danny couldn't take it anymore. He picked up the phone and dialed his mom.

"Can I speak to Eileen Torbert, please?" he asked the person who answered the phone.

There was suddenly a commotion in Dad's office. Danny could hear the sounds of tumbling furniture and breaking glass.

How could he still be on hold? Why hadn't Mom picked up yet? Phone at his side, Danny ran to the office door and pushed it open.

Rick and Steve were fighting. Both stopped and stared at the boy.

Danny's voice cracked. "Dad? Are you okay?"

Steve was the first to move. He grabbed the

phone at the desk and pressed the talk button. With Danny's handset on, there was no dial tone. In fact, the muzak from the bank's hold line was blaring out of the speaker.

"Who did you call, Danny?" Steve screamed in Danny's face. He threw the phone against the wall. "Who did you call?" He backhanded Danny across the face, knocking him against the wall.

As Danny slid to the floor and raised his hands to protect his face, Rick screamed and hurtled the coffee table at Steve. The table exploded across Steve's chest and sent him flying backward. Rick rushed Steve and punched him, again and again. Steve wrestled free, his face swollen and bloody. Suddenly, he dove toward his briefcase.

As if in slow motion, Danny watched his father lunge at Steve, to stop him from doing whatever he was doing. But Steve was out of his grasp. Steve turned around, slowly raised his hand, and aimed his gun at Rick. Then he fired. Over, and over, and over again.

Danny knew he screamed. He opened his mouth so wide, his lips cracked. He felt it tear his throat on the way out, but he couldn't hear it because of the thunder of Steve's pistol.

His father's limp body crumpled to the floor.

Danny knew what was next. Still numb from the beating and the sight of his dad's body, he got to his feet.

Time returned to normal.

Steve rolled to his side and fired, but Danny was already out of the office.

Through the kitchen, around the corner, to the back door. Danny heard an explosion from the gun and something splintering behind him. He yanked the back door open and stepped one foot into the backyard. Then he heard the gun shot and felt something thrust his body through the doorway.

He felt weightless. Then, he felt nothing.

Two weeks passed before Danny regained consciousness. And it wasn't until more than a month later that he could wrap his brain around exactly what had happened.

His mom told him that the doctors had kept him sedated throughout the surgery, the transfusion, and the first ten days of recovery. Paramedics had revived him at the house. He lost the lower lobe of his right lung and would need months, maybe years, of therapy to regain his strength.

A couple of weeks later, a tutor came to Danny. He brought make-up work from school and would be Danny's teacher for the next several months so that he wouldn't have to repeat sixth grade.

Because of his injury, Danny was most interested in the human anatomy lessons from his life science class. He absorbed all he could about the vital parts of the body and what he would need to do to take care of them. Danny later understood that these same vital parts were an enemy's weak points.

In physical rehabilitation sessions, Danny had to exercise and lift weights. He hated every minute of it. His body strength was drained. His mental strength wasn't there at all. He just didn't care.

Of all the sessions, he hated group counseling the most. Sitting in a circle. Sharing feelings. It was a little too much like being on *Oprah*. Get in touch with your feelings; set yourself free. He knew his feelings would not set him free. His feelings would chain him to the bed and never let him see the light of day again. Guilt overwhelmed him – he had waited too long to call his mom. Why had he hesitated? If he had listened to his first instinct and called his mom, the police could have been there in time to save his dad. Instead, he had burst into the room with the phone in his hand. Steve knew that he had called for help, so that's why he attacked him. His dad only attacked Steve because he had hit his son. Steve shot his dad because his dad attacked him. The entire thing was all Danny's fault — through his own actions, he had caused his father's death. And his killer had still not been found by the police.

No matter how the counselors tried to explain it to him, Danny believed that he was just as guilty as Steve. His father was murdered and there was nothing Danny could do to bring him back.

Several months into his rehabilitation, Danny was getting into the routine of it all. However, one afternoon as everyone was leaving their group counseling session, one of the other patients lunged at Danny and tried to stab him. Some orderlies had managed to restrain the patient, whose name was Jorge, while another orderly rushed Danny to a secure room.

Jorge had only been part of the rehabilitation center for a few days. In the course of their investigation, the police discovered that Steve had sneaked Jorge into the center to kill Danny, who was the only witness to his crime. After a long interrogation session, Jorge told the police where they could find Steve. Steve was then arrested and in police custody within the hour.

After the incident, Danny was whisked out of the hospital in a minivan to another hospital many hours away. There, his mother and someone named Mr. Lankford from the FBI talked to him in private. Mr. Lankford explained that as a witness to Steve's crime, Danny was in danger. Also, because both Danny and Eileen could identify Steve's criminal associates, they were both in danger. Steve wanted them both dead, and he had the power and influence to make that happen, even from behind bars. The FBI wanted the Torberts to testify against Steve in court so that they could put him in jail for a long, long time. Mr. Lankford explained that Danny would have to tell the court about everything he knew and everything he had seen that day. Although Danny knew it would put their lives in even more danger, he could not handle the guilt that weighed like lead on his shoulders. He agreed to testify in court. Mr. Lankford gave the mother and son information about new identities, new lives, and new beginnings. But inside, Danny knew the truth: You can't hide from yourself.

The trial was quick. Eileen, Danny, and Mr. Lankford testified. Eileen explained that although Rick's phone had been broken, Danny's handset had still been connected and she had heard everything from her desk at work. Danny relived every moment of that horrifying day. Mr. Lankford gave background information on the case, stating that the FBI suspected Steve of terrorist activities. Unfortunately, because there was not enough proof – Steve had destroyed all of the surveillance files that proved his guilt – Steve was only convicted on the charge of murder, and not on the charges of terrorism. Steve was sentenced to life in prison, but he made it very clear that the first chance he got, he would appeal.

Despite the fact that Steve was behind bars, Danny and Eileen were still not safe. Steve's associates were still on the outside, and would no doubt try to hunt them down. With Mr. Lankford's help, Danny and Eileen became Dylan and Nicole in Colorado. Then, they were Zack and Kate in Tennessee. With each new incarnation, there was always a problem, a fluke that put them in jeopardy. No longer trusting anyone, Mom convinced Mr. Lankford to give her computer equipment so that she could generate their identities herself. That way, she would only have to contact him if absolutely necessary. Mr. Lankford gave them the freedom they needed to move in and out of identities, like spirits. He gave them life, even though Danny didn't feel he deserved it.

* * *

As Danny — now Alex — stared at the article breathlessly in his classroom, he could feel the guilt enveloping his heart and creeping back into his lungs. He knew he had killed Mr. Lankford too.

CHAPTER 13

"ALEX," TIM WHISPERED as he quickly glanced at the paper. "What's wrong?"

History class came back into focus. Alex was standing, and everyone was staring at him. "I, uh ... " He couldn't form words.

Thinking fast, Tim interjected, "Mr. O'Neil, Alex is gonna be sick all over the place. Can I get him to the nurse?"

"Yes, by all means. Alex, are you okay?" The teacher stopped them as they walked by. "I'll call the nurse and tell her you're on the way."

Safely out of the classroom, Tim shuffled Alex into the closest bathroom. As Alex squatted and put his head between his knees, his friend checked under the stalls.

"You ready to tell me what's going on yet, Alex?" Tim waited, but received no answer. "Does this have something to do with the dead cop?"

Alex didn't move a muscle. He was trying to make the cold sweat, the fuzzy vision, and the high-pitched squeal in his head go away.

Tim refused to let Alex off the hook. "I'm your friend. You can talk to me." He paused for a minute, but still no response. "By your reaction, this guy must have been a relative of yours?" His eyes widened with realization. "Or you're in some kind of trouble. Is that why you get quiet sometimes and act funny?"

Alex tilted his head to look at his friend but had to drop it again when the fuzz returned.

Taking that look as a confirmation, Tim blurted, "What can I do to help?"

Alex spoke from his tucked position, "Nothing, we'll be all right."

"Nothing? How can you say that? Dude, I'm your friend."

"Yeah, and I want to keep it that way. So just stay out of it and don't mention this to anyone, okay?"

"Stay out? I'm already in this."

"No you're not. So leave it alone, or you'll be dead too."

Tim was silent.

"I can't tell you anything," Alex said, picking his head up and dropping it back against the bathroom wall. "Not yet anyway ... And really, by the time – " He cut himself short before he could say anything else and closed his eyes.

"What?" Tim prodded. "You'll be gone? Is that what you were going to say? Is that why you guard everything so well? You move every time there's trouble?"

Silence.

"You've got to quit running sometime!" Tim was yelling now. "I'd like to think that your friends here mean enough for you to make this your home."

Alex locked eyes with Tim. "My friends are important enough that I don't want them dead."

A second later, the door rattled. "Alex? Tim? Are you all right? I'm coming in." The nurse opened the door to see Alex still crouched on the floor.

Alex shot Tim a panicked, pleading stare. *Please, Tim. Help me.*

"He couldn't make it down the hall. We came in here to get some water on his face." Tim's eyes never left Alex.

Alex looked up at Tim and knew that he could trust him with anything. Maybe even with his life.

* * *

When the phone rang at the pizza shop, Alex's mom assumed it was another pick-up order. Bonnie yelled, "Sonya, phone's for you!"

She almost dumped the broccoli cheese soup in her customer's lap. *What's wrong? No one knows I'm here, except ... Alex!* In her mind, a million disasters happened to her son on her way to the phone.

Bonnie gave a baffled look as she handed her

the receiver.

"Hello? This is Sonya."

"Hi. This is Mrs. Layton, the school nurse. I'm afraid Alex is sick. He's all cold and sweaty – I think he's been vomiting. Can you come pick him up?"

"Oh, thank God!"

"Excuse me?"

"Oh, I mean, yes. I'll be right there."

* * *

In a small, windowless room lit by fluorescent tubes, a happy computer geek typed away on his computer. The underpaid National Security Agent, whose name tag identified him as Ed, was earning his retirement money early.

He had first met Frank on the job maybe two years ago. Seemed nice enough. Frank started bringing Ed some side work and paid him with huge sums of cash. A week ago, Frank gave him another assignment: find all contacts associated with Tom Lankford of the FBI. The amount of money promised to Ed was even larger than normal, probably because of the FBI connection, Ed figured. No biggie – hacking was his job and he was good at what he did.

Ed worked in the world's largest surveillance center, Echelon, where the United States, Canada,

Australia, New Zealand, and England worked together to check all emails, faxes, phone calls, and text messages for threatening information. There were certain keywords like "bomb" that were his usual targets, but Ed could change the target words to anything he wanted, like "spaghetti," "Jessica Simpson," or "Witness Relocation Program."

When one of these keywords popped up, it took Ed little time to trace the message back to the exact computer, phone, or device from which it had come.

With dollar signs in his eyes, Ed modified the search procedure a little. He started with Lankford's workstation, followed all incoming and outgoing messages to their servers, and located every workstation on the other end.

On Wednesday at 11:18 a.m., while Alex was lying in the nurse's office, Ed made an unmonitored phone call.

"Frank, I've got the addresses. Now you bring the money."

CHAPTER 14

ALEX REFUSED TO speak until they were in the car.

His mother opened her mouth, but Alex beat her to it. "Mom, Mr. Lankford's dead."

"What?"

"It was in this morning's paper. They shot him!" he yelled. In the last couple of years, his mother had never known her son to lose control. He always put on an outward show of strength and composure. But now, he was completely freaked out. "They know! We're in trouble! We have to leave! We – "

"Okay. Just a minute. Calm down," his mom cut in. "How do we know it was Steve?"

"Because I can feel it."

"Okay. First I need to see this newspaper. Let's see exactly what it says before we go crazy."

"Crazy? We've relocated for a lot less than this," Alex insisted. "We need to move."

They were silent as they pulled into the driveway of their townhouse. They didn't speak again until they were safely inside.

"Okay," his mom continued once the door was

closed. "Just think about this for a minute. Even if they did kill him, he didn't tell them anything ... He didn't know anything. The only communication I've had with him in the last two years has been through e-mail. And I stopped doing that at least two moves ago. Nobody knows where we are."

"Still, our one protector is dead – murdered," Alex argued, but much quieter than before. "And we're left waiting for somebody to find us."

"No, we've taken control of our lives. As long as we don't do anything to attract attention to ourselves, we're as safe as we've always been."

Alex held back his gut response: *That's supposed to make me feel better?* He couldn't say that to his mom. She was trying so hard to make him feel safe. He chose instead to say, "I guess you're right. I'm sorry I freaked out."

"You don't really want to leave here, do you?"

"No. I like this place."

"I can tell," she smiled weakly. "I like it too. Let's stay for right now. But let's be sure to keep our eyes open."

* * *

"So what exactly does this crap mean?" From across the visiting table, Steve waved away the papers Frank held in his hands.

"It means that we know where Eileen was when she last contacted Lankford. We traced all of Lankford's contacts to their computers' addresses. Eileen's were the only ones that moved, which means that she's the only witness who has moved. With a little more research, we could sell the locations of the other witnesses to the felons they helped convict," Frank boasted.

"I don't care about that," Steve snapped. Then the businessman inside him added, "At least not yet. My appeal date is less than two months away. Come March 1st, I want no living witnesses." The anger was back in his voice. "Understand?"

"I understand."

"Good. So where are they *now*?"

"We don't know. We're hoping she tries to contact Lankford's office when she sees the headlines."

Steve couldn't believe his ears. He kept his voice low, but his mouth nearly foamed with fury. "Let me get this straight. You try to get the information from Lankford, but you can't, so you kill him. Then I pay some computer geek $200,000 to do all this paperwork, and we still don't know where they are?"

"No, but there's the – "

"Shut up!" Steve glanced at the security guard, who started walking his way. Steve made eye contact, shook his head, and gave a fake grin at the guard. The guard gave a warning look and walked back to his post. He continued much more quietly. "I'm not waiting for her to contact them. She hasn't in over a year, and she'd be stupid to do it now."

Frank nodded in agreement.

"Where are the girls?" Steve continued.

"They are just about done with Maryland."

"This is going way too slow. I only have a month and a half left until my court date!" Steve checked his voice level again. He leaned in closer to Frank. "It's time for a different approach. Use your government contacts to get into the social security files."

"That's a different department. It's not going to be that – "

Steve's glare was enough to stop Frank in mid-protest. "They moved in November," Steve explained, as if to a two-year-old. "So if Eileen began working in November or December, the social security office would have a record of a new number appearing in that state. Check for a single parent with a newly-enrolled child at a nearby school."

"But there's millions ... and we don't know

which state."

"Then you shouldn't be wasting your time talking to me." Steve leaned back in his chair. The conversation was over.

With that, Frank stood and walked out of the room. He could feel Steve's glare burning a hole in his back all the way through the gate.

CHAPTER 15

FOR A WEEK and a half, Alex pretended nothing was bothering him. He was getting better at it each day, but there was still a nagging feeling in the back of his head – he could feel it right behind his left ear – that something was really wrong this time. He decided to be the good son and let Mom believe he was fine. He would bury his guilt over his dad and Mr. Lankford. He would pretend to be a skateboarder named Alex. And he would be prepared to run at any moment.

He felt more fake and exposed than ever.

To make him feel a little safer, his mother bought them each a new cell phone for emergencies only. She paid with cash, used different names, and bought prepaid cards. There would be no connecting the phones to the two of them. She set her phone number on his speed dial and vice versa, and that made him feel better.

"The key," she reminded him, "is to go on as if nothing happened. If you start acting paranoid, you'll attract attention."

Therefore, when Tim started giving him the silent treatment, Alex figured he was just being paranoid.

He decided it was all in his head and that he would just go along as usual.

That Saturday, Sonya drove the boys to a salvage yard in search of a rail – "so we can grind!" Nate had repeated about ten times. After over an hour of hunting, they found an old, eight-foot, galvanized steel pipe. They drove immediately to Tim's house with the pole sticking out diagonally from the back window of the Toyota, which caused a lot of stares.

Tim politely thanked Alex's mom, but hardly said two words to Alex.

The boys worked for a few more hours elevating one end so that it resembled a handrail on stairs. Then Nate, of course, was the first to ollie up and execute a 50-50 frontside grind. He landed the trick and thrust his arms in the air in victory. "Gnarly!"

Everyone clapped and grabbed their boards.

Alex celebrated the completion of the group project by keeping a promise to himself. He walked to the top of the ramp and set his board's tail on the edge. *No skill here*, he encouraged himself. *Just guts*. He stomped his front foot on the board and went down. On his first try he bailed. The board slid down without him.

Just guts, he told himself. On the second try, he dropped in.

Nate and Tyler applauded. Tim said nothing.

* * *

They met all week immediately after school and held sessions on the completed half-pipe and rail. None of them cared that winter had finally arrived and the temperature plunged into the thirties. Tim's mom had to pry them off the ramp each night after dark.

One Friday night, Tim, Tyler, and Nate agreed to meet right after breakfast the next morning to skate. Alex, however, had to decline. "I can't come tomorrow. Will you guys be here on Sunday?"

Tim gave him a look.

"What are you doing?" Tyler asked with a slight attitude.

"There's something I gotta do with my mom." Alex gave his best eye-roll for effect.

"We'll be here Sunday," Nate said grabbing his bike. "See you guys tomorrow."

"Wait up," Tyler yelled pedaling after him.

Tim looked at Alex when the other two were out of earshot. "Will you really be here on Sunday?"

Alex understood his meaning. "I'm not leaving, Tim. There's just something I've gotta do tomorrow."

"What?"

"What do you mean, 'what?'"

"I mean," Tim said, "*what* are you doing tomorrow?"

"I told you, I'm going somewhere with my mom," Alex defended.

"Why do you always have to be like this?" Tim flung his arm in frustration and took a step back.

"Like what?"

"Like *this*!" Tim said much louder. "You give me a lot of half answers and obvious lies. You don't even mention that day in history class when you freaked. What's going on with you?"

"Nothing's going on," Alex assured. "I just freaked that day in history. But I think I've got it worked out. I'll be here Sunday," he repeated.

Tim nodded. After a moment, he offered, "You know, if you need my help with whatever ..."

"Yeah, I know." Alex looked down. "I hope it doesn't come to that ... Thanks though. I'll see you Sunday."

* * *

Gina walked down the steps of Pocomoke High School. Their search in Maryland was complete. She and Leah would meet tonight in Baltimore to discuss beginning Virginia on Monday. Gina planned to continue traveling down the East Coast and then sweep west. She thought Leah should start in the Fairfax area and then travel south.

Gina made a mental note to tell Frank to cross Maryland off the social security number hunt. Danny wasn't in Maryland, and there was no way Eileen would send him to school in one state and work in another. She wouldn't be close enough if something happened.

She sighed to herself as she took the barrette out of her hair in the car. *Ballantine had better come up with a big bonus for this one, because this search feels like a total waste of time.* Some of their clients in the Midwest were getting impatient, and armed extremists were not people she wanted to make angry. Aaron was in Minnesota now, trying to satisfy some of the customers, but he needed help. Gina and Leah should be helping Aaron, not wasting time looking for the boy and his mom. Steve was ruining the business and endangering all of their lives by fixating on them.

It was time to get rid of Steve. Aaron could certainly take his place. Gina knew she wouldn't make a good leader; she was too hot-headed. She didn't mind killing people, but it was usually a spur of the moment decision. However, Aaron was smart and ruthless. He would do whatever it took to get the job done.

She sighed again as she drove toward Baltimore. She would see how this quest went. If they didn't find the kid by the time they covered South Carolina, she would have to talk to Frank and Aaron about mutiny.

At the next light, she checked her PDA. There were over fifteen high schools in the Norfolk and Virginia Beach area alone. *Fifteen!*

She wanted to kill someone right now.

CHAPTER 10

ON SATURDAY, SONYA and Alex made a short trip away from town. They traveled past the school and into a rural area very different from the Virginia Beach suburb they were now used to. They turned off the road at the third mailbox with a blue burglar alarm sign attached. Neither spoke as they drove about 300 yards along the twisty, bumpy dirt path, which led them to a large barn-shaped house with a two-story garage next to it. An old, dark blue Chevy Blazer sat in the driveway.

Alex got out of the car. He could see nothing but trees, some of which had blue and red paint splattered on them. He listened. Other than the loud purr of Mom's car, there were only forest sounds. One word popped into his head: *secluded*.

"Have a good time, honey."

"I will," he said, glancing around to see if anyone heard. Mom should have known not to call him that when there could be other kids around.

"Call me when you're ready."

"I will." He shut the door and gave her the customary half-wave as she turned the car around and slowly left the driveway.

He turned to see Brian walking up behind him.
"Good. You found the place."

* * *

The boys rode four-wheelers through the woods for two full hours. Alex didn't know how to work a clutch very well at first, but he got the hang of it. On one section of the path was a clearing. They got the Yamahas up to 60-something mph, but not the 80 mph they had hoped.

"Wow! That was cool!" Alex proclaimed, taking off his helmet back at the house.

"Yeah, I thought you'd like it," Brian said with the first real smile Alex had seen him show. "I think we should jump some ditches next!"

"No, that's okay. Casts make me itch. Hey, do your parents own all these woods?"

"My dad does. My mom lives in Pittsburgh. There's thirty-two acres – Dad likes his privacy."

"That's for sure. I couldn't hear a thing – no trucks, no sirens, nothing."

"Yeah, it's quiet. You want lunch?"

"Definitely," agreed Alex.

The kitchen confirmed that Brian's mom didn't live there. There were no flowers on the hand towels. The placemats had Harley Davidson logos on them.

Things were neat, but in piles. Alex missed the typical "man" stuff in his own home.

"The bathroom is the second door on your right if you want to wash up."

Alex looked down at his mud-crusted hands. "Okay, thanks."

Alex noticed a small, gray box wired to the phone on his way down the hall. *Weird*, he said to himself.

Brian's dad came in a little later for lunch. He was a tall, slightly heavy man with long hair and splotches of oil from head to foot. "Hi," he said. "You must be Alex. I'm Brian's dad." He continued wiping his hand on his jeans. "You can call me Ron. Sorry about the grease."

Brian stared at his dad and hinted, "I thought you were going to be working on your truck."

"I *am* working on the truck," Mr. Joseph replied, staring back. "I just came in to get a bite to eat. Why don't you go get cleaned up?"

Feeling a little uncomfortable, Alex tried to break the tension. "Hi, Ron," he said, accepting his greasy handshake. He wasn't used to calling friends' parents by their first names and it felt odd. "I love the woods on your property."

"Thanks. I like space, and I don't have to worry about not liking my neighbors."

Alex smiled. Still scanning around the room, he

noticed a lump near Mr. Joseph's ankle. "Thanks for letting me come over. I really like the four-wheelers."

"Yeah, Brian and I race 'em all the time. He's learned how to fix 'em too."

Brian left for the bathroom.

Then Mr. Joseph whispered, "I'm really glad you came. Brian has been talking about you since you moved here. You've really made an impression on him."

"Uh, thanks," Alex said quietly, shifting his eyes to the floor.

"No, I mean it. Ever since you stood up for him, he's been a different person. And I wanted you to know I appreciate it."

Brian returned, and Mr. Joseph changed the topic back to racing four-wheelers.

* * *

After lunch, Brian suggested they go to the garage. "I've got something else to show you," he said.

Brian led Alex to a large wall cabinet. He snapped open the doors and revealed several strange pistols.

"Guns? Are these yours?" Alex asked. Guns made Alex nervous.

"Yep! They're paintball guns. They're awesome!"

Alex smiled faintly. "So you run around the woods and shoot trees?"

"No, I use the trees for practice. So, you want to try?" Brian asked with hope in his eyes. "We'll use the fresh paintballs, not the frozen ones I use for target practice. They're like marbles – they would take your head off."

All he really wanted to say was, *No thanks. This is a little too real-life for me.* But instead, he shrugged and said, "Sure." Alex was impressed by how sincere he could make himself sound. "And my head thanks you!"

Brian handed him padded camouflaged clothes and a face mask. "Is all this necessary?" Alex asked.

"Yeah, the balls sting really bad if you don't have pads on, and the goggles..." He then said in his best grouchy old lady voice, "You could put your eye out with that thing, Sonny."

Brian gave him the basics, and they spent the next hour or so stalking each other through the forest. As the bright blue paint smeared on his gear proved to Alex, Brian was an excellent shot.

When Brian went in the house later to grab some sodas, Alex stayed in the garage to peel off his gear and call his mom to pick him up.

"I want to thank you again for all you've done

for Brian," Mr. Joseph repeated as Alex hung up the phone.

"It's okay," Alex said, brushing off the compliment. "I really didn't do anything that I wouldn't have done for anyone else."

"Yeah, but even those losers he usually hangs around with didn't try to help him with the firecracker thing," Mr. Joseph stated. He caught Alex looking at the lump on his leg. "Are you wondering about this thing around my ankle?"

Alex's face burned. He had already figured it out. The telephone box and the lump on his leg were probably parts of an alarm system he'd heard about in the hospital. Mr. Joseph was on house arrest.

Mr. Joseph hiked up his pant leg to show the black band and small silver box attached to his ankle. "I was drinking one night after work, and I decided to drive home. The dumbest thing I've ever done. I hit a girl who tried to run across the road."

Alex nodded.

"I got ten years. They let me out after three, and I'm under house arrest for two. I can go to work, the store, and home. Anything else, I have to call and get permission first. If I step out of these woods without phoning in, I go back to jail."

"Dad!" Brian had walked in and stormed away in embarrassment.

Alex went after him. "Brian, really, don't worry about it."

"This is all I need," Brian grumbled holding his head. "My dad's going around telling my friends he's a convict."

"Dude, it's okay. People make mistakes. I'm not going to tell anybody."

"Don't you get it?" Brian asked. "If people find out he's been in jail, people will ... I might as well move!"

"Look, Brian, at least you have a dad."

The sentence was out of Alex's mouth before he could stop it. Maybe it was the lunch conversation. Maybe it was the father-son engine tuning. Maybe it was the Harley Davidson placemats. Alex slipped. He had always been careful. His face burned with embarrassment.

Brian stared at him in shock.

"I'm sorry, Brian." Alex wished his face would turn back to its normal color. "That just came out. Uh ... wow ... My dad ... died ... a few years ago, and I've been thinking a lot about him recently ... And ... "

Brian stared.

Alex continued, "I'm sorry ... And if you give me a hug, I'll slug you."

Brian flashed the faintest of smiles at Alex's joke. "Okay then." Instantly serious again, he added, "I'm really sorry about your dad."

90

"Yeah," Alex whispered. "Um look, I really don't like to talk about that, so if you could ... just ... not tell anybody I told you that ... "

"I won't," Brian said. "And you won't tell anybody about anything here, right?"

"Deal," Alex agreed quickly.

He hoped he hadn't revealed too much.

CHAPTER 17

ED WAS SURE that Frank was Satan. He could remember his grandmother telling him, "Boy, you go makin' a deal with the devil, you're gonna get burned." She was so right.

That two hundred thousand was sweet. Ed had set up an account with a little bank in the Philippines, where he planned to retire as soon as he had confirmation that the money had been transferred to his account. However, before he could catch his plane, Frank appeared again and made him an offer: either hack into the social security and IRS files or explain to a judge why he sold government secrets to known criminals. Ed thought immediately about running, but that was not an option: Frank and some tall, thin guy always seemed to be parked outside his house, the grocery store, everywhere. Ed had sold his soul, and Frank held the receipt.

On an untraceable machine in a dark cellar office at Echelon, he worked for the devil. Ed hunted social security codes that newly appeared in Virginia and the Carolinas during November. Then, he had to cross check those numbers with tax dependents entering schools in the same states. This job would be so easy in April, after everyone filed their taxes, but no one keeps the Devil waiting.

Ed punched in code after code with so much anger, the "A" and "S" keys began to jam. Swearing at himself, Ed unplugged his keyboard and replaced it with another one from the office. At least that made him feel better.

Three hours later, after two weeks of work, Ed finished Virginia and found just over thirty single parents with only one child that were new to the area in November.

He'd call Satan later and tell him about his progress so far.

* * *

"Genetic variation."

"Right, Brian," praised Miss Jenkins. "And who can name another factor in population survival? Debbie?"

Go Brian, Alex thought. Maybe Mr. Joseph – Alex still felt weird about calling him Ron – was right. Brian did seem like a different person. He didn't turn into a nerd or goody-two-shoes or anything, but he had made some changes.

"What's up with Brian?" Tim whispered, covering his mouth with his hand. "Did he eat a science book for breakfast?"

Alex smiled. "Maybe he couldn't find anybody's lunch to steal."

Tim grinned, but he too had noticed that Brian hadn't been punching kids or throwing anyone in the dumpster all week. Something was up.

Alex had already slipped back to daydreaming about paintball. It was bizarre, but thinking about trying not to get shot took his mind off of trying not to get shot.

* * *

"We have had three new admissions since November. One girl in the sixth grade. Two boys in the eighth," Ms. Wisniewski said.

"I'm trying to get a fair cross-section of students," lied Gina, speaking as a Virginia Department of Education employee, for the fifty-thousandth time in the last week. "I have recently interviewed three girls and several African American students. Is either boy Caucasian?"

"Yes, one is," stated the secretary in a half-laugh, knowing how ridiculous state reports were when it came to race and gender. "I have his school ID card information, and I can bring up his picture on the screen here in just a second."

When a window with the student's information and photo opened on her computer screen, Mrs. Wisniewski's voice was a touch triumphant.

"There you go. Alex Miller from Ann Arbor, Michigan."

"Thank you." Gina smiled. "I think he'll be perfect."

CHAPTER 18

THE LOUDSPEAKER BEEPED. Then Mrs. Wisniewski called, "Miss Jenkins?"

"Ye-es," the teacher replied in the two-syllable, singsong voice that everyone seems to use when answering loudspeakers.

"Could you send Alex Miller to the office, please?"

Alex's heart stopped. Thoughts sped through his mind. *What could they possibly want? Maybe Mom is on the phone. Maybe she's hurt. No. They would come to the door and ask for me quietly. Maybe they found out I'm not Alex. Maybe –*

"Sure, he's on his way. Alex, leave your books, and bring me your hall-pass notebook."

Outside the classroom, Alex scanned the hallway for anything strange. His heart pumped so much adrenaline, his body tugged at him to run straight through the front doors, but he resisted. He could feel every hair on his neck standing at attention, as if they too wanted to bolt out the front door.

He turned the handle to the office to see Mrs. Wisniewski at her desk, talking on the phone and scribbling something on a form. She held up her index finger to indicate that he should wait a minute.

A tall brunette sat in a chair to his right. He noticed she had a leather notebook and a nice pen, which she held like a cigarette.

"Alex," Mrs. Wisniewski said as she put down the phone. "Miss Reynolds is here from the Department of Education. She is interviewing new students in the state to see how our schools meet their various needs. We selected you at random to answer a survey."

The adrenaline burst into Alex's head like a wave of lava. *Selected? Survey? Interview?* He calmed down a little at the word "random," but his neck hairs were still telling him to head for the door.

Gina extended her arm. "Hi, Alex. I know you want to get back to class as soon as possible." She smiled at her joke. "I just have a couple questions, and I'll be out of your way."

He nodded and swallowed softly. That sounded encouraging, but did she seem a little anxious, or was he being paranoid?

They walked to the copy room, where a couple of teachers were drinking coffee and teasing each other about something Alex couldn't quite catch. They eyed the newcomers and began whispering.

"Okay," Gina sighed. "First of all, I want to thank you for your help. This is an anonymous survey, so your name won't be included in any way.

We just want to find out how we can improve our school system to accommodate students like you from other areas."

Alex liked the anonymous part. But he felt she was really looking him over. He tried to look her in the eye, but she was busy looking at his hair, his ears, and his chin. Once, he thought he saw her staring at the right side of his chest, as if she could see the scars beneath. When she finally made eye contact with him, she gave a brief startled look as if she were caught. She was studying him.

"Where did you move from?"

"Ann Arbor, Michigan." Alex stated his standard lie too quickly. He was showing that he was nervous. *Get a grip*, he told himself.

"I like that town. I used to visit college friends there," she said. "Did you ever eat at Café le Chat?"

Trouble. The warm feeling returned. He had never even been to Ann Arbor. *Is she testing me or being nice? Stick to the basic lie. Don't add to it.* "No, my Mom and I don't go out much, except to McDonald's."

"Okay." She looked disappointed and scribbled something. "Comparing your former school to this one, were your classes in Ann Arbor (a) easier, (b) more challenging, or (c) about the same."

"About the same," he answered. It seemed as

good an answer as any.

"What level math did you take at your former school?"

"Algebra."

"And do you take that course here?"

"Yes." He noticed she picked up her pace. She was done studying him and was ready to leave, he guessed.

She asked him several more questions about his old school and his move here. She asked the questions quickly, and Alex returned his responses just as quickly.

She closed her leather folder and extended her hand. "I'd like to thank you for your time, Alex." Then, pausing only to soak in his face one more time, she left the room, thanked the secretary, and walked out of the building briskly.

Alex looked at Mrs. Wisniewski. "Is that all she does all day? Surveys?"

"I guess," the secretary replied. "You'd be surprised what they pay people to do."

Alex watched as Gina pulled her white Buick out of its parking space rather quickly for someone who was driving in an area filled with children. The whole situation felt wrong. Paranoid or not, he needed to get out of there. He patted his left pocket, but he remembered that his phone was in his backpack in his classroom.

"Mrs. Wisniewski, can I use your phone?"

"Is it an emergency, Alex?"

Yeah, lady. I think that woman who was just here is part of a plot to hunt me down and kill me, Alex thought. "No, but my mom would like to know I've just been singled out for a survey that she didn't know about."

"Well, then tell her tonight and have her call if there's a problem," the secretary declared, holding her hand over the phone. "Give me your pass, and I'll sign you back into class."

"Okay." He handed her his pass. He had to get out of there.

* * *

As soon as Gina was out of eyesight, she pulled over to the curb. Nearly dropping her phone in excitement, she found the number she needed in her directory. "Frank? I've got him."

CHAPTER 19

ALEX FLASHED HIS pass as he walked past the hall monitor and surveyed the area for an easy exit. He spotted the clock. 11:48. In two minutes, his class would be dismissed and the halls would be full of students ... and teachers. He would have to time this just right. He slid into the bathroom.

Ripping a page out of his hall-pass notebook, he scribbled a note. He folded it in quarters and placed it in his left palm. He stuffed his pen and a couple more pieces of paper into his pocket in case he needed them later. He went back into the hall.

The hall monitor nodded his way as if to say, "Hi, I see you. Now get back to class."

Alex returned the nod and walked at a leisurely pace to his class. He had less than a minute to kill.

As he entered the science hallway, the bell rang. The doors flew open and students were everywhere. Alex slid along the row of lockers and avoided the bulk of the mob. He appeared behind Tim and slid the note into his friend's hand.

"You didn't see me come back," Alex whispered.

Tim's eyes grew round as he understood. Silently, Tim handed Alex his backpack, which he had picked up before he left the room. Alex took out his sweatshirt and his phone and returned the backpack to Tim.

"Can you hold this for me?" Alex asked his friend, but he didn't wait for an answer. Alex disappeared into the mob, keeping his head low so that he wouldn't make eye contact with any of the teachers.

Tim casually went to his locker and grabbed his English book. He opened the note and read:

Tim,
I hope you meant what you said, because I think they found me. Please go home after school; I'll try to call you there. Don't tell anyone. I hope I'm wrong.
Alex

* * *

Alex slid out the side door next to the foreign language hallway. Since he wasn't taking a language, the teachers wouldn't know who he was. He just needed to make it to his bike.

He slid along the school wall, below the windows, as quickly as he could. When he reached the fire exit doors, he had to stop and check for teachers. The coast was clear, so he scooted past the door and to the bike rack.

He undid his Kryptonite lock and hopped on his bike. It occurred to him that there was no way he was going to get out of the empty bus parking lot unnoticed. There were too many windows. *If I'm wrong, I could get an in-school suspension*, he thought. *If I'm right, I could get killed.* There was no choice. He pedaled as fast as he could across the asphalt.

* * *

"We just landed in Chicago, but we can be on another plane within the hour," Frank explained. "The plane to the Virginia Beach airport will take another three hours. We'll call you as soon as we land. Are you sure it's him?"

"I'm not positive," Gina replied. "But I've studied his picture so much, I see it in my sleep. The eyes, chin, and smile all match. And he was acting jumpy, like he had something to hide. I really think it's him."

"We'll let Ed keep working through the data files until we're certain. I'll hook my laptop into the plane's phone system. E-mail me if there's a problem. Whatever you do, don't lose him."

"Impossible. I got his address off the computer screen when the secretary showed me his picture," Gina stated proudly. "When he gets home, we'll walk in and grab both of them."

"Fantastic, but watch the school anyway. We can't let him slip by like he did in Colorado."

"I'm already in position," she assured him and pushed the "End" button on her cell phone. Now all she had to do was wait. In four to five hours, this would all be over and she could finally go home and relax in time for the weekend. She spun the lid off her thermos and poured some maté tea into her cup. She took a small sip and coughed the tea all over her dashboard.

To her right, she saw Danny dart out of the school parking lot, across two lanes of traffic, and down a side street on a bike.

"That little punk!" Gina yelled as she started her car and pulled into traffic. He was not going to ruin another weekend.

CHAPTER 20

ALEX PEDALED HARD down the street. He just wanted to put some distance between himself and the school.

He turned onto a side street and pulled over to call his mom. However, he didn't have a chance to get the phone out of his pocket.

A car squealed past the intersection behind him. He glanced over his shoulder to see the white Buick speed by, driven by the woman he had just met at school. Their eyes met for just an instant as she slammed on the brakes and turned the car around.

Alex pedaled faster than he ever had before. He leaned hard to the right to dodge a honking car at the next stop sign. His pursuer swerved the Buick around the car, gunned the engine, and barreled toward him.

Alex tried to gain some ground by turning at every intersection that came his way, eventually coming full circle to where he had first spotted the Buick. He was getting tired, but the car was still coming. He had to change the rules, and he had to time it right.

He drove straight through the next stop sign and let the car close the gap between them within several yards. He locked his back brake and skidded 180 degrees onto a driveway and then the sidewalk. He pedaled like a madman as the car, in turn, locked its brakes and slammed into reverse.

He cut through someone's yard and rode across the lawn, through another yard, and onto a parallel street. He could hear the Buick's motor revving into gear and turning the corner.

He quickly pedaled across the next yard before she could see him. He stopped next to an aluminum shed and dropped flat on the ground, bike and all. He had to wait to see where she was going.

* * *

When she realized she had lost him, Gina cursed loudly to herself. "Forget Frank! When I find that little jerk, I'm just going to run his butt over and ID the body later!"

She pulled her car off to the side of the road and shut the ignition. He couldn't be far away. She had been chasing him for about fifteen minutes. He had to be tired, and if he coasted to rest those legs, his 10-speed bike would make that loud clicking noise she remembered from her biking days. All she could do was listen.

"Hey you! What are you doing in my yard?" Some woman down the street was ranting, and Gina knew she had found him.

"Gotcha," Gina said and turned the key.

* * *

The screen door flew open and an older lady with a broomstick hobbled toward him. "Hey!" she screamed, swinging her weapon high. "What are you doing here? This is private property! I'm going to call the cops, and I'm going to come over there and – "

Alex didn't wait for her to finish. He scrambled back to his feet and ran the bike to the next street. He saw the Buick pulling up to the street across from the yard. As he jumped on the bike, he could hear the car turning the corner. He hoped his adrenaline could hold on for just a few more minutes.

He decided to try his trick again. He knew his body was not going to last for much more, so this was going to have to be it.

As the car gained on him, he could tell she planned to run him over. Cutting it too close, he swerved into the next driveway as the Buick careened onto the sidewalk, barely missing him and taking out the brick mailbox instead.

He pedaled up the long, curved driveway and looked back to see Gina get out of her wrecked, steaming car. He smiled. Then his mind went blank as he realized that he was heading straight into a fenced-in backyard. He was trapped.

* * *

"You're mine, little brat!" she fumed. He was pedaling straight into a fenced yard. *Like shooting fish in a barrel*, she thought. She grabbed the 9 mm from under her seat, and as she strolled up the driveway, she attached the silencer.

This was her prize for all the trouble this kid had caused. She checked the clip and flicked off the safety. She had it planned: one in the head and two in the chest. She would take no chances.

She rounded the driveway to see a beautifully landscaped patio and pool, but no Danny.

* * *

Danny heard the click, click, click of heels coming up the cement. Scan. Scan. The way he came was the only opening to the yard. He tried the door to the house. Locked. She was getting closer. He had to get over the fence.

Scan. Scan. Pool, diving board, slide ... slide. *Bingo*. He raced to the slide and climbed as fast as he could. Click, click, click. From the top of the slide, he leaped and grabbed at the top of the fence. Pain shot through his hands, but he pulled himself up enough to get his foot on another spike. He heaved his way up and as he scooted his other leg up and over the fence, he vaguely felt the blood dripping from his hands. He didn't pause to look for his hunter. He quickly and quietly climbed down the cross braces to the wooded lot on the other side.

The clicking of her heels slowed as she realized that he wasn't there. He panicked for a minute, but then he remembered her high heels. She wouldn't be following him over the fence.

For a few minutes, he ran through the trees, crossed two roads, and then had to slow down. He was exhausted. Looking down, he saw the blood and his ripped clothes and realized that he needed to lie low. But he had to reach his mom. She was in danger too.

* * *

Gina seethed. She checked the doors, which had security stickers stuck all over them. Locked. She checked the shrubbery. No luck. Then, she noticed a smudge of blood, high on the fence by the pool. *That little weasel got away*, she thought. *But he's hurt.*

She took off her shoes and ran back to her car. She had to get out of there before the cops showed up. A few people were coming out of their houses to see what all the commotion was about.

Too many witnesses. She needed a ride. She smiled to them as she grabbed her notes, silencer, and phone and stuffed them into her duffel bag.

One nicely dressed man approached and asked, "Are you okay?"

She covered her head and faked disorientation. "I think I have a concussion. Some kid tried to carjack me. Can you drive me to a doctor?"

He helped her to his Audi, which was parked in a nearby driveway.

Situations like this were the reason she always rented her cars under false names. She would change her clothes and wig shortly, since the witnesses would obviously give her description to the police.

She relaxed and enjoyed the ride for a couple of minutes with the handsome man, who was the only witness to get a close look at her. She'd wait until they were a few more miles away before she killed him.

CHAPTER 21

AS SOON AS the "No electronic devices" sign went out, Frank checked his messages. He was annoyed to learn that Danny had escaped. Gina had informed him that she had another car and was on her way to Danny's house.

Frank had mixed emotions about Gina finding Danny. He was glad that the boy ran, because that made it clear that this was the kid they were searching for. But still, they had left Ed alive, as a backup. This meant that once the Danny mess was over, he would have to fly all the way back to Echelon to kill the computer geek. Steve would flip out if he knew they had kept Ed alive. Frank sighed. This was going to be a long day.

He tapped the passenger in the seat next to him to show him the message. Aaron, apparently asleep, lifted his head and his sunglasses long enough to read the screen. He smiled. "Got him," he whispered. "Tell her to just hold them until we get there. We need to make sure there are no other loose ends we need to tie up." He returned his head to its resting place.

Frank sent Gina a brief message. Then he

checked to see how the stock market was doing.

* * *

Alex surveyed the damage. He had two large splinters and a cut between his right forefinger and thumb. His left hand hurt, but there was no visible injury. He hoped it wasn't sprained. His sweatshirt and T-shirt were both ripped across his stomach. Underneath, his stomach was scratched, but it wasn't bleeding much. He tore the T-shirt where it was ripped, to make a temporary bandage for his hand. He couldn't walk around bleeding all over the place.

His hips hurt, but he realized it was from pedaling with a pen in one pocket and a cell phone in the other. He removed the phone and hit the speed dial. His breathing became short and choppy as the phone rang.

His mother answered on the third ring. "What's wrong?" He had never called her cell before this.

"Mom, they found us. We've got to leave."

"WHAT? What happened? Are you okay? Where are you?"

"They found me at school." His voice was frantic. He could barely keep from yelling, let alone slow his words down. "Some lady was taking a survey and I got suspicious. I skipped out and she tried to run me down."

"She *what*? Are you okay?"

"Yeah, I cut my hand, but I'll be all right. Can you come get me? We've got to leave – *now*."

"Where are you?"

"I'm in some development with woods behind it. I know I must be a few blocks from Great Neck. How about I meet you at the convenience store at the corner of Great Neck and First Colonial?"

"Good idea. I only have about a hundred bucks on me though. I'm going to have to stop by the house. It's on the way to Great Neck."

"Forget it, Mom. They probably already know where we live."

"I'll be careful. Besides, we won't make it too far on a hundred bucks."

"Okay, but don't get anything else. We really have to get out of here!"

"I'll be there within fifteen minutes."

* * *

Six minutes later, his mother approached their driveway. She saw no unusual cars or people hanging around. She reluctantly turned off her car, since the house keys were on the same ring. "Just get the money and leave," she said to herself. She opened the car door.

Still wearing her waitress apron, she walked up the sidewalk. She tried to see into her house as she walked, but it was useless. She always kept the curtains closed. She jiggled the key to make it fit in the lock and then turned the knob.

She breathed a sigh of relief when she saw no one sitting in the La-Z-Boy facing the door. Wasting no time, she went into the bedroom closet and grabbed the old Reebok box with the money and social security numbers – her "running box."

She spun around and started out of the room. She barely felt the butt of Gina's gun hit the back of her head.

CHAPTER 22

GINA TYPED, "I'VE got Eileen" into her cell phone. When she had adequately gagged and tied up Alex's mom and stuffed her in the trunk of her Audi in the garage, she hit "Send."

"Good," came Frank's reply almost immediately. "Sit on her for two hours until we get there. If Danny shows up, try not to kill him yet. Aaron is looking forward to that."

"What if he decides to run?" she wrote back.

"He won't leave without his mother. He'll call soon. Give him these directions."

* * *

Alex arrived at the convenience store ten minutes after his phone call. He went immediately to the bathroom to wash up and try to look presentable. The bleeding had just about stopped on his right hand, so he took off his makeshift bandage – it drew too much attention. He balled up a paper towel and closed it inside his fist to catch any stray drips that hadn't yet clotted.

He bought a Pepsi so that he wouldn't look too

suspicious, then headed back outside.

It had been fourteen minutes since the call.

Three minutes later, he started getting those paranoid twinges again. He walked away from the parking lot to avoid feeling like a sitting duck. He found a good place, in a row of trees separating the store from the house next to it, where he could see the whole parking lot. He sat down and waited.

Twenty minutes and over thirty checks of his watch later, he knew she wasn't coming. She would have called if she were merely delayed. He debated whether he should call and risk detection, or wait until he heard something. He decided he couldn't wait – he had to know.

He punched the speed dial. The phone on the other end rang twice.

"Hello?" It was a female voice, but not his mom's.

"I need to speak to Sonya."

"Well, Danny," she said, dropping her voice to a lower pitch. "This *is* Danny, right?"

His head exploded with heat and panic as he realized his worst fear had come true. They had his mom. He should have tried harder to convince her not to go home. He should have known better. He *did* know better, but he let her go anyway. She was either dead or close to it, and it was his fault. Again.

117

"I'll take that as a 'Yes,'" the voice continued. "You see, your mom can't talk to you right now, she's in the trunk of my car."

"Is she alive?"

"Yeah, she's alive, but not for much longer if I don't see you, Danny." He could hear her smiling through the phone.

"Like you really plan to just let her go if I show up," Alex, now Danny once more, blurted sarcastically.

She continued, "Well, she has a better chance of living with you here, than she does without you. Are you willing to take that chance?"

Danny said nothing. Of course he wasn't willing to take that chance. He had to do everything he could to save her. Even though it was obviously a trap.

"Now, you just bring your little butt home and we'll handle this quietly."

She was still at his house! Although he was stupid enough to get into this situation to begin with, Danny was smart enough not to go home. He had seen enough movies to know that situations like these should never be settled in a secluded place. It was safer to keep it public. There was less of a chance that she would shoot him with a lot of witnesses around. "No."

"What?" she asked, not believing her ears.

"Maybe I should just take care of things now."

"You might have already," he said flatly. "Let me talk to her."

"Ooooh," she returned. "Has someone been watching crime shows on TV? Sure, you can talk to her."

Danny heard a chair creak, which he assumed was the La-z-Boy in the living room. He heard footsteps echoing in the kitchen, followed by a click and then the faint creak of the garage door. He heard keys rattle and slide into a lock, and then there was a hollow thump as the trunk latch popped open. He heard a ripping noise, which he assumed was tape being torn from his mom's mouth.

"Alex?" His mom wouldn't betray him, even at the cost of her own life.

"Mom!" He wanted to say he was sorry. He wanted to say he'd try to save her if he could. He just wanted to talk to her. He didn't get the chance.

"Okay, that's it!" announced the female voice.

Danny heard a slapping sound, which he hoped was only the intruder putting the tape back on his mom's mouth, followed by a loud clunk as the trunk was slammed shut again.

"That's all you get, Danny. I think it's adorable how she still calls you Alex," the voice mocked. "So are you coming or what?"

"You've got her locked in the trunk?" Danny yelled.

"She'll be all right as long as you show up." Gina paused. "Well, what's it gonna be?"

Danny's thoughts whirled. He had to go, but that would be suicide. He needed a safe place. "I won't come there," he stammered. Tears were just a breath away and he knew she could tell. "It has to be somewhere public."

"There's that TV influence again, Danny. Where would you like to meet?"

Good question, he thought. "We need to meet on the boardwalk."

"Hmmm. I don't know. I'll have to call you back," she teased. "Oh and Danny, I'm outta here as soon as I hang up, so don't bother calling the police. If you do, you know what will happen." The line went dead.

Danny paced. That was stupid. How was he going to get to the boardwalk? He should have said a parking lot, like on TV. No, too many parked cars. There could be a sniper in any of them.

A sniper? Danny had an idea.

* * *

Five minutes later, Danny's phone rang. He answered on the first ring.

"Hello?"

"Danny." The female voice sounded cheerful — too cheerful. Something was up. "We'll meet at the miniature golf course on Pacific and 16th at 5:15."

"That's not on the boardwalk," Danny objected.

"Tough! You didn't think I'd actually let you dictate the terms, did you?" she snapped. "Here's the deal: You'll be standing alone at the golf course. We'll drive up and you'll get in. Your mom will be in a different car, so if you do something stupid like call the cops, that's it."

"I'll need to talk to her before I get in any car."

"You'll get to," she insisted. "And don't be stupid, Danny." She hung up.

I don't plan on it, he thought.

CHAPTER 23

DANNY NEEDED TIME to think. As he walked toward the beach, he tried to piece all of his ideas into a solid plan. There had to be a way out of this mess. Calling the police was an obvious solution, but he knew Steve's thugs would kill his mom. What had he been thinking? The beach on a cold February afternoon was not going to be very crowded at all. It wasn't a sunny weekend as it had been just a few weeks ago when people were off work and cruising around. Plus, it would be getting dark by 5:45. Could he use the darkness to his advantage? Were they planning on doing the same thing?

He checked his watch. 3:38. He punched the numbers on his phone.

"Hello?"

"Tim?"

"Alex, where are you? Are you okay?"

Danny started shaking. "Look, I'm in trouble. I hate to get you involved, but I don't know what else to do. They've got my mom."

"Who?" Tim asked with disbelief. "*Who's* got your mom?"

Danny took a big breath. "It's a really long story,

but here's the short version. The man who killed my dad is trying to kill me, and his goons have grabbed my mom. If they don't see me at a certain time, they're going to kill her."

Tim said nothing.

"Tim?" Danny asked. "Are you there?"

"I'm here," Tim assured him. "I'm just trying to put this all together. I knew something was up, but I didn't really – "

"I know this is a lot to dump on you, but I need help. In about two hours, I have to meet with these people, or they'll kill my mom."

"Dude, they always say that," Tim said. "If you go, they're going to kill you too – " He stopped himself.

His friend just admitted what Danny already knew in the pit of his stomach. They would kill his mom whether Danny showed up or not. And then they would kill him too.

"I think you've got to call the police," Tim pleaded.

"I can't. They'll kill her."

"Then what are we going to do?"

Danny smiled faintly. Tim knew the risks and he was still willing to help.

"I need some help with the area by the beach, and I need you to do a couple things. Do you have a piece of paper?"

Tim grabbed some paper and started writing

everything down. He only interrupted Danny once to say, "Aw man, why?" Then he let Danny explain. They discussed the layout of the beach area and after he thought about it, Tim made some suggestions too.

As Danny made his way to the beach, his ideas gelled into a plan.

* * *

At 4:48, Frank and Aaron pulled into the parking lot of the McDonald's in separate cars. Inside, they met Gina, who was already finishing a salad and a medium order of fries.

"You guys want something to eat?" Gina asked, slurping the last of her soda.

"No," Aaron said. "I'll wait until afterwards. I want to go over this again."

"Eileen still in the trunk?" interrupted Frank.

"Yes," Gina, who was now blond and was wearing jeans, assured him. "Don't worry, I have her wedged in with the spare tire, so she can't flop around and make a bunch of noise. She's got enough air 'til we need her."

"Good," Frank nodded.

Aaron began rehashing the plan. "Gina, you drive my Mazda around first and check for cops. I'll follow in your car."

CHAPTER 24

5:10. **DANNY DIDN'T** like it. There were fewer cars in the miniature golf course's parking lot than he had imagined. He had planned on there being at least a little rush-hour traffic.

And most of the skateboarders and roller bladers had gone home. The sun was setting quickly. It would be dark in another twenty minutes. In addition, the wind was picking up off the ocean and it was getting really cold.

Shivering inside his ripped sweatshirt, Danny figured he'd rather be cold than dead. So he rubbed his hands together and decided he'd better get focused. The dark would be his friend, he told himself.

From his partially obscured waiting place next to the giant gorilla on mini-golf hole number two, Danny watched a green Mazda go down the street for the third time. This was obviously one of Steve's men, checking out the area for Danny and police. Danny could barely make out a figure inside, talking on a phone.

"Yeah, I'm right here, jerk," Danny mumbled. He was so nervous, he wanted to throw up. Danny watched a couple of hardcore skateboarders ollieing off the sidewalk across the street and he felt a little better. "Are we going to do this or what?"

On its fourth circle around the avenue, the Mazda pulled up to the curb and stopped across from Danny. A blond stepped out and remained at the driver's side with the door open. She spoke over the car with an icy tone. "Hello, Danny."

Danny recognized the voice – and now the rest of the features – of the woman who tried to kill him a few hours earlier.

"If it were up to me, I'd shoot you now," Gina declared.

Danny stood motionless.

"Look," Gina continued, reaching in to her jacket. Danny tensed. "Here's the deal." She pulled out her phone. "Your mom will be here in a minute. You'll get to see her and then you need to take a ride and answer some questions."

"Yeah, answer some questions," Danny repeated. "Is that all?"

Gina said, "That depends on how well you answer the questions."

If I get in that car, I'm dead, Danny thought. He chose to simply nod.

Gina spoke into the phone, and a blue Audi pulled up from a side street and to the curb directly behind the Mazda. A tall man stepped out and walked around to the curb.

Danny felt his heart speed up. He recognized Aaron immediately.

Those soulless eyes brought back all of those nightmares that had terrified Danny when he was eleven. Danny was older now and he refused to hide under the covers anymore.

"Get in," Aaron commanded.

"Where's my mother?"

"We'll take you to see her."

"No, I need to see her first, or you'll have to shoot me here," Danny bluffed, raising his arms out to the side in defiance. He edged a little closer to the big gorilla statue. He knew Aaron wouldn't shoot him there because there were passing cars and still a few skateboarders around. *These people are afraid of witnesses*, Danny reassured himself. That is why Danny and his mom were being hunted. And that is what would now keep him alive.

Aaron showed no emotion. Without taking his eyes off of Danny, he nodded to Gina, who spoke into the phone.

Two blocks down, a gold Honda Accord entered Pacific Avenue from a side street and pulled about twenty feet behind the Audi. Frank got out and walked around to open the door for Danny's mom so that she could briefly stand next to the car. Her hands were bound and Danny could barely see a gag. In a split second, it was over. Frank pushed her back into the car and returned to the driver's seat.

"Danny," Aaron stated quietly. He opened his jacket with his left hand. There was a pistol inside a shoulder holster. Then he opened the passenger door. "Get in."

From the direction of the Honda, a rider-less skateboard rolled down the sidewalk toward Aaron.

Danny stayed mostly hidden behind the gorilla. He was pretty sure it wouldn't stop bullets, but it made him feel a little safer. "Hey, Aaron," he blurted, trying not to sound as scared as he was. "I wonder what's on the skateboard."

Aaron looked at the skateboard. Something small was duct taped to the top. In black Magic Marker, someone had scribbled "Check out this video" on the duct tape.

Aaron lifted off the duct tape and removed the small package, which was a cell phone. He hit the buttons to play the video. Danny knew that Aaron was watching the recording of himself signaling to the driver of the Honda. Then he watched as the video showed Danny's mother, gagged and bound, being shoved into the back of a car.

When Aaron looked up, Danny had a little more

control of his voice. "Well, what do you think?"

"I think you should get in the car."

"Really?' Danny glared at him in astonishment. "I thought you would ask something about what's going on."

"No." His eyes were as empty as Danny remembered. "I don't care. You took a video and now I have it. Get in the car." He stepped toward Danny and put his hand on the pistol.

"Whoa!" Danny yelled. "You're missing the big picture."

Aaron grabbed Danny's arm and pulled him toward the Audi. Gina came closer to help, but Aaron clearly didn't need it.

Danny panicked. This wasn't the way it was supposed to go at all. He had to get through to Aaron somehow. "There are more cameras, Aaron."

Aaron talked while he dragged the boy. "By the time the cops are here, we'll be gone."

"Cops?" Danny twisted to stare into those empty eyes. "Who said anything about cops?"

Suddenly, he had Aaron's attention. "What are you talking about?"

"I'm talking about the Internet," Danny explained. "I'm talking about posting this on CNN, BBC, YouTube, MySpace, and pretty much anywhere that will let us post this video for the whole world to see."

Aaron briefly gave him a puzzled look then shoved Danny against the car.

"Sure, the police will look for you," Danny grunted. "But I figure the terrorists you work for will find you first."

He had Aaron's full attention now.

"I figure terrorists don't want any publicity. They won't stand for anyone who could attract the police to their operation – no one who could possibly sell them out to save his own skin. And with the millions of witnesses who will see you stuff an obvious hostage into a car, you, Aaron, are a problem. Now, *I* know you would never rat out your associates to the police." Alex's voice strengthened as he became more comfortable with his role. "But do you think your terrorist buddies will take any chances? They might think you're a leak, so they'll probably have to plug you." Danny hoped his little joke made him sound sure of himself. "I don't think there would be anywhere in the world where you could hide."

Aaron stepped back from the boy. "So what are you offering?"

"The footage, in exchange for my mom and me."

Aaron seemed to consider this. "How about if I kill you now and then find your little friend with the skateboard and kill him too?"

"Do you think you can find him faster than he can hit 'Send'?" Danny looked directly into Aaron's eyes. "What do you think? You let two witnesses go, and you avoid two million other witnesses."

Aaron didn't agree. But, Danny noticed, he hadn't pulled out his gun either.

"Think about it, Aaron," Danny pushed. "You let us live, we let you live."

"Let's just shoot him now," Gina demanded.

The hatred in Aaron's eyes nearly burned a hole in Danny's face.

"Deal," he said to Danny at last. "Give me the other camera."

Danny was surprised by Aaron's quick agreement. He must have realized that Danny could – and did – have another camera. But he was releasing Mom and that's what mattered. "Untie my mom and give her a thirty-second walk toward the beach," Danny insisted. "I'll get the camera for you."

Aaron's face was stone.

"What's the worst that could happen? I have no video and you shoot me right here?"

Stone.

Finally, Aaron flipped his phone open and dialed. "Frank, release Eileen. Shut up. I'll explain later. Tell her to walk toward the beach."

Moments later, Eileen was out of the car and

walking across the miniature golf course toward the beach. Danny's eyes followed her until she was out of sight.

After thirty seconds, Aaron said, "Well?"

Danny nodded. With Aaron at his side, he walked back to the gorilla statue and picked up the camera that was resting in a shadow on the gorilla's hand.

"Here ya go."

"Is this it?" Aaron punched the buttons and watched part of the video.

"That's it. Are we good?"

Aaron nodded. "I'm good." He grabbed Danny's bleeding hand, twisted it behind his back, and yelled, "Frank, kill the woman."

132

CHAPTER 25

EILEEN WAS BEYOND confused. She saw Danny talking to Aaron and it made no sense. By any form of logic, she and her son should be dead. Then Frank untied her and told her to walk toward the ocean. She ran. She had expected a bullet as soon as her back was to him. When there was no shot, she stopped running and turned around to try to see what Danny was doing. Why was he still with Aaron? Was he trading himself for her? She couldn't let her son do that.

She heard a loud whisper. "Mrs. Miller." Tim was at her side. "Come with me, now!"

"But Danny – "

"He's fine," Tim said. "Come on!"

She ran. Then she heard Aaron's voice: "Kill the woman!" She sprinted. Past the amusement park, onto Atlantic Avenue. There, Brian and his four-wheeler were waiting for her.

She turned to Tim, but he was gone.

"Hop on!" Brian yelled and gunned his engine.

* * *

Aaron thought for a moment. There must be a trick here somewhere, but he couldn't see it. At first, he thought the boy had outmaneuvered him. But now, Aaron had the camera, the video, the woman, and the boy. He couldn't see the downside here. Even if there was another camera around here somewhere, and he assumed there was, he knew people who could alter the videos he now held and put it on the web to disprove whatever copy Danny might still have. He would muddle the facts and hide the truth. Misinformation. Wasn't that what the cell leaders paid him for? Well, that and killing people, which he planned to do now.

"Gina, we're out of here," he ordered, as he pushed Danny onto the car again. He didn't have time to enjoy Danny's grunt of pain. This whole operation had taken nearly seven minutes. He couldn't risk this taking any more time.

His phone rang.

"Aaron, she got away!" Frank yelled in his ear.

"What?"

"I'm not waiting around for – "

Aaron didn't catch the rest. Something was rapidly pelting the car, denting the hood, breaking the windows. *Bullets. No. Marbles maybe?* He ducked as he shouted orders. "Gina! Take care of those shooters."

* * *

Danny thought he had heard the roar of Brian's four-wheeler and he felt some relief. Mom should be safe. Now he had to get away. He hoped Nate and Tyler were paying attention.

When the frozen paintballs hit, Danny pivoted off the car to sprint away from Aaron. Flying from the balcony twenty yards away, the paintballs would only distract the killers for a moment. He barely had taken two steps when Aaron grabbed him. He yanked Danny's head backward into his chest. "I never liked you, Danny," the assassin hissed, shoving a silenced barrel under Danny's throat.

Danny's right hand had already found his weapon. He thrust his right arm behind his back and buried his Bic pen into Aaron's upper thigh. He missed the artery he was aiming for, but he heard a cry from Aaron. Danny jerked his head backward and to the right to avoid the gunshot he knew would follow.

* * *

Aaron felt the pain shoot through his leg and up his spine, into his face. He pulled the trigger as a reflex, but also out of anger. He was vaguely aware

135

that he missed the little brat as he dropped his head to check his leg.

Aaron screamed and clutched the pen still lodged in the muscle of his inner thigh. He ripped it out and cursed. With his left hand, he pressed hard against his thigh to stop the bleeding. With his right, he raised the pistol to kill the little punk.

He caught only a glimpse of the black grip tape from the skateboard before it smashed into his nose. Aaron's head hit the cement and then he blacked out.

* * *

"Aaron!" a woman's voice screamed.

Danny turned to see Gina sprinting toward him from across the street. He ducked behind the car. Moving as low and as fast as possible, he slid around the Mazda and then the Audi, in order to keep a barrier between him and Gina. Danny eyed the gorilla and the trees beyond to calculate whether he would have enough time to run onto the golf course, which would provide better cover.

He didn't like his chances. And out here in the middle of the street, he had little cover.

He heard Gina cock her pistol.

Then, he heard the sweetest sound in the world. Sirens blared as a swarm of police cars pulled onto both ends of the street. Guns were drawn and there was a lot of shouting. And after all of her icy anger, Gina let herself be handcuffed.

Danny didn't watch the whole arrest procedure. He picked up the camera from the sidewalk and walked toward Tim's hiding place in the shrubbery next to the golf course.

"Thanks for the cops," he told Tim.

His friend came out and grinned. "Sometimes you just need to call for backup." He handed Danny an open phone. "It's for you."

Danny grabbed it. "Hi, Mom. Yeah, I'm okay."

With his adrenaline gone, Danny could barely move. He dropped where he was and sat on the sidewalk. He closed the phone and looked at Gina and Aaron in the police cars. He nodded to Nate and Tyler running across the street toward him. He was too tired to wave. When he heard the sound of Brian's engine again, he smiled. His friends had stood with him, and his mom was safe. At last, some of the guilt that had weighed him down had lifted.

Feeling much lighter, he stood and walked toward his friends. It was time they had a talk.

CHAPTER 26

FUMING, STEVE BALLANTINE sat alone, high up on his usual bleacher seat during his recreation time in the Illinois prison. He was a respected ruler, and he expected his commands to be followed to the letter.

He shook his head. He couldn't believe how badly his crew had botched the job. It was planned perfectly. Get one little kid – what was so hard about that? Incompetent idiots. Aaron and Gina were in jail. They deserved what they got. That was the price of failure.

Luckily, both Frank and Leah had been smart enough to escape and lie low. As soon as it was safe, they would contact him, and then they would track Danny down again. Steve's parole hearing was approaching. He knew there was little chance of the board releasing him after this fiasco. Still, there was the next parole date to plan for.

Marcus was the first to sit down next to Steve. His friends followed.

Steve didn't hide his resentment. "Is there something I can do for you?" Steve reprimanded, puffing up his chest. Marcus knew the rules. If he wanted

Steve to arrange information or supplies, he had to be discreet. Usually he slipped Steve a note with a shopping list. He never brought friends.

"Yes, there is," Marcus said as he smiled to a guard. "I saw an interesting video."

Steve stiffened. "Hey, that mess didn't involve me."

"But it involved your men," Marcus continued calmly. "We are all only as strong as our weakest link."

Steve turned red. "My weak links have been replaced. Even now, the rest of my crew is restructuring to meet whatever needs you may have."

Victor, sitting behind Steve, whispered, "I doubt that." He lifted his wrist briefly to show Steve a sharp metal object tucked in his sleeve.

Steve, formerly a lion, sat quietly, knowing his brief time as a deer had just begun.

* * *

Frank's three-week-old scruff may have been enough to disguise him, but he wasn't taking any chances. Like Leah beside him, he had changed his hair color and style. Their colored contacts and tanned bodies completed their disguises. They walked smoothly out of the airport and past the palm trees toward their rental car.

Frank felt free for the first time in weeks. After a lot of moving around, they had chosen a long-term hideout. He and Leah would stay in Saba for the week to look for a place to buy with the emergency money his crew had stashed away before they were all thrown in jail. He figured they wouldn't need the cash anytime soon. He and Leah wouldn't be returning to the United States. They would live here forever with enough money to relax and put the past behind them.

They would start a new life.

From binoculars many cars away, their killer watched them get into their car. He double-checked the pictures on the seat next to him as he screwed the silencer onto his pistol. Then, he followed them to their hotel.

* * *

Danny burst into the house. "Mom, I'm going to Tim's. We're going to skate until dark."

"Okay. But remember, Danny, dinner is around six thirty!" she yelled from the bedroom.

In the three weeks since everything had happened, Danny and Eileen had shed their disguises. It was time to be themselves and create real lives, not new identities. Their cover was as blown as it could get. All of Steve's known associates that posed any threat were in jail, except for one.

"And this time, try not to lose Ben," his mom said.

When the Torberts decided not to relocate after the attack, the FBI provided guards for Danny and Eileen, at least until the trials were over, or until they found the last killer, the one they only knew as Frank. The Torberts both identified Frank in a series of surveillance photos from the Illinois prison. The FBI was searching and had contacted foreign govern-ments, but there had been no sign of the fugitive.

Danny flipped his hair out of his eyes and smiled at the plainclothes officer next to him. "Okay Ben, but maybe you should get a skateboard instead of the car."

"Yeah, I'll have to do that," Ben said.

The last weeks had been rough. The police had interviewed them at least a dozen times. Lawyers called to schedule court appearances. Danny and his friends must have uploaded the video to every site that would let them. With a simple video editing program, Danny was able to fuzz out the faces of anyone in the video he didn't want the world to recognize. He wanted them to recognize Frank.

The upcoming weeks didn't promise to be

much better. There were school records to set straight with the district. There were social security numbers to iron out with the IRS. And there were all sorts of other identifications to resolve with banks and state departments.

Somewhere along the line, Danny and his mom would have to steal some time for themselves. They needed time to sit back and realize that after a very long time, the Torberts were the Torberts again. Danny and Eileen needed to figure out exactly what that meant.

For now, it was time to stop running. But biking, four-wheeling, and skateboarding were fair game.

Danny threw open the door and jumped on his skateboard, as Ben tried to keep up.